UNBOUND I
LOST FRIENDS

UNBOUND I: LOST FRIENDS
EDITED BY DOUGLAS OWEN

Science Fiction and Fantasy Publications
http://scififantasypublications.com
An imprint of DAOwen Publications

Unbound I: Lost Friends
Edited by Douglas Owen

ISBN 978-1-928094-04-3
EISBN 978-1-92094-05-0

Jacket art: Aleksandra Klepacka

10 9 8 7 6 5 4 3 2 1

Welcome to the first Unbound. Science Fiction and Fantasy Publications' flagship theme based anthology focusing on the talents of Science Fiction and Fantasy story tellers.

This anthology is a dream of our editor, who has been a lover of the written since he first learnt to read. The old Science Fiction anthologies of the 1940's to 50's were lent to him by his grandmother, and they captured the young boy's heart and imagination. It was the only common ground he enjoyed with this father's mother.

Unfortunately the collection of anthologies his grandmother enjoyed has long disappeared, along with her collection of "Adult Fantasies" as she put it. But the love of those stories was passed along.

We at Science Fiction and Fantasy Publications hope that you enjoy the enclosed stories just as much as we enjoyed bringing them to you. Each has a unique look at the theme of lost friends, and the authors are from different parts of our small world. It took 5 people to choose the stories you are about to read. Many people submitted, only these authors were found worthy to be included in print.

As you read each story, please decide which one is your favorite and post on GoodReads. We would like to see if your thoughts agree with our staff.

Again, thank you for purchasing a copy of the anthology and we look forward to hearing from you.

Sarina Dorie

Her work can be found in multiple magazines. Sarina won the Penn Cove Literary Award three times, the humour category in Allasso 2 and the best fiction in Allasso 3. Her novel, *Silent Moon*, won 2nd place in the Duel on the Delta contest and Golden Rose contest. As well as 3rd in the Winter Rose and Ignite the Flame contests. Sarina is a talented story teller but an accomplished novelist. Look for her upcoming novella, *Dawn of the Morning Star*, due in 2016.

The Waking of Sleeping Beauty

I was seven when I had what the psychologist calls my "traumatic experience." Some kids accidentally walk in on their parents in the bedroom and are scarred for life. Only when I walked in on my mom, the man with her wasn't my dad. And what they were doing was far worse than any sexual act.

The TV repair man was no stranger at our house. The holoscreen acted up once a month. I did wonder why we just didn't get a new one, but my dad never questioned it. When it wasn't the TV, it was the stereo, and when it wasn't that, it was the smart oven or the computer system. Though, being only seven, I couldn't imagine why Drew, the repairman, and my mom locked the bedroom door and spent so long in there.

Drew was kind of old, always wearing coveralls, not the kind of guy you would imagine Rachel Yamasaki, former model and Miss Mars would be interested in. But he was nice enough for a gaijin, or non-Martian. Sometimes he showed me how to take electronic toys apart to rewire them and make them do tricks, and he always gave me candy, even when my mom protested. He teased me when he came over and told me I was going to grow up and become a ladies' man, and though I didn't know exactly what that meant, I decided I liked him.

One day I was home, sick with the flu, and taking a nap in my room. I woke up, calling for my mom to see if she'd bring me some of her homemade miso soup. When she didn't come, I got out of bed. Our house was modeled to look like an ancient Japanese home with fake tatami mats and walls made of rice paper, however, the walls were actually soundproof plastic covered in rice paper. I stood in the hallway calling her, kicking at the bamboo plants in annoyance.

Her bedroom door wasn't locked, so when I opened it, I got a good view of her on the bed, back to me. Her black hair was up with ornamental kanzashi in it and she wore the same house kimono she'd worn earlier, only it was obviously untied as the robe was slipped halfway down her shoulders.

Drew was sprawled out on the bed next to her. He wore his work coveralls and tapped away on his laptop. It took me a second to notice what was amiss. A bunch of wires from his computer were plugged into a panel in her neck and upper back, lights flashing, metal and wires exposed. She had some kind of metal earplug in her ear with blinking red lights—probably the reason she couldn't hear me. In the fraction of a second it took

2

me to view this weird, science fiction horror scene, they both turned to look at me. Immediately, Drew pulled the plugs out of her neck and ear. She straightened her kimono, tied it amazingly fast (an inhuman feat in itself) and glided toward me.

I was too frozen with terror to move. My mother was a machine, a . . . robot? It wasn't like I didn't know about their existence. We'd been to some Senator's house who had a robot butler. And every Saturday on our way through the biosphere park to get to the Shinto temple, we saw women in short skirts who my mother said she felt bad for and I'd overheard her call them "sexbots." But most of the robots I'd seen had been on the holoscreen. They looked like us but had glowing, red eyes and usually went on killing sprees. If robots short circuited as often as our holoscreen did, I couldn't blame my father for wanting us to walk as far away as possible from the bots in the park.

My mom kneeled beside me and felt my forehead like nothing had happened. "How do you feel, sicky bear? Do you still feel pukey?"

I shook so hard I couldn't make my voice work right away. My eyes filled with tears and I burst out, "You're not my mommy!"

The warmth in her brown eyes faded into something resembling pain. "Sammy, I am your mommy. Do you feel afraid right now? You know Mommy wouldn't ever hurt you, right? And I wouldn't ever let anyone hurt you. Just because I'm an android doesn't mean I love you any less." She scooped me up in her arms and kissed me. It took a few more minutes before I stopped crying. She asked, "Do you want to see what Drew and I were doing?"

"Okay," I said. My fears lasted about as long as

my attention span.

Drew looked a little wary, but he opened the panel in the back of my mother's neck and plugged her back into his computer. I sat on the bed, and tucked myself under the plum blossom comforter, mesmerized by the blinking lights. It was kind of pretty.

"I'm programming more recipes into her hard drive. And you've begun to study Japanese-Martian history this year, so I'm adding some general knowledge about the early days of colonization so she can help you with your homework," Drew explained. "I also do a routine maintenance check when I come over."

I smiled, pleased by the idea no one else had an android for a mom. Not that I knew of anyway.

After a few minutes, it became pretty boring and my mind began to wander. "Is Daddy a robot, too?"

Mom squeezed my hand. "No, he's human."

"Am I a robot?" I felt the back of my neck. I couldn't feel anything different, but the back of her neck had looked normal when the panel was closed.

"No, you're human, too."

Too bad. It would have been handy to be programmed history instead of having to study it for hours at school. "Does Daddy know about you?"

She leaned over and kissed my brow like she always did. "Oh, yes. He was the one who had me commissioned."

"Huh?" That was a pretty big word. Though I got the gist of what she was saying, I didn't understand.

She ruffled my hair, messing it up. She looked to Drew. "I think I should take him to see the original Rachel Yamasaki."

•   •   •

I was surprised to learn my biological mother was locked in a spare bedroom in our condo. She lay surrounded by pale blankets and blank walls, her blanched face blending in with the white room. Her dark hair and bruised eyes were the only color in the room.

My first thought was that this was sleeping beauty. Only this woman wasn't beautiful. Scars adorned her sunken cheeks. Blemishes and wrinkles marred her face. Her limp hair lacked luster. She was hooked up to machines, tubes coming out of her arms and face. She was far more mechanical looking than my mom.

Mom sat on the edge of the bed, her eyes flickering to the monitor on the wall. "Hello, Rachel, it's me. I brought someone to visit you today, our son. Say hello, Sammy."

"I'm not the prince," I said, afraid I might have to play the part of Prince Charming. "I'm not kissing her."

"I didn't ask you to kiss her. But perhaps someday when you're grown up, you'll wish to show her affection. And while you are here, I expect you to be polite and respectful. Many doctors believe coma victims can hear conversations and have sensory awareness even though they're asleep. We can give her comfort and reason to wake up. I used to bring you here when you were a baby so she could hear you, but Daddy asked me to stop when you turned two. I still see her every day when you're at school and tell her about you."

I stared at this Frankenstein-like mother in the bed. Hoping she couldn't hear me, I whispered, "She's so ugly."

"She's flawed and therefore perfect in a way I'll never be," Mom said, her smile wistful.

I scrunched up my face trying to understand this logic.

"She is wabi-sabi, the beauty of imperfection," she said. "It's like the story of the monk who comes across a serene garden in the autumn when the maples are red, the bamboo neatly lined up and hedges trimmed, and the Zen garden stones forming even, parallel lines. The beauty is flawless and too perfect, therefore the monk shakes a branch on the maple tree, causing a single leaf to fall. The garden is then perfect in the wabi or imperfection, and he enters."

I rolled my eyes. She so didn't get it. This was the weirdest day of my life. I'd just found out my mom was an android and this deformed twin was tucked in a secret room — and my mom wanted to tell me stories about Zen gardens and monks.

I pointed to the imperfect sleeping beauty. "But why is she so ugly? Why doesn't she look like you?"

Mom smoothed the hair out of my eyes. "I was designed to look like her when she was twenty-two, right before her accident. You see, she was in a shuttle that crashed and got hurt very badly. But your daddy loved her so much he couldn't stand the idea of not having Rachel with him, so he secretly commissioned me to be built in her likeness to take her place, as well as serve as her nurse. The programmer did such a good job with the personality programming, no one knew the difference.

"Your father was my owner and I was programmed to be loyal to him and love him alone. But after a while, your daddy wanted to have an heir. He asked a doctor to help him make a child using Rachel's DNA and his DNA and put it inside my belly. But Drew, my programmer, felt that it was more important to make sure I loved you, too, so with Daddy's permission, he changed my programming to make you the owner and person I cared about more than any other."

In the movies, robots could only have one owner and robots had to listen to them. In my favorite episode of Batman and Totoro, everyone found out Mrs. Kitara was a robot because she had two owners. When she tried to please both of them, but couldn't because they wanted different things, her program overloaded and her head exploded. It was supposed to be funny, but Mom never laughed when I watched it.

About this time, I thought my brain would overload from all this information. It must have shown on my face because Mom asked, "Do you want peanut butter and jelly sushi for dinner tonight?"

•   •   •

During dinner my father asked, "So, how was your day, Samuel?"

I looked up from the plate of peanut butter and plum jelly sushi waiting at the center of the low, kotatsu table, my reward if I finished my miso soup. The lines of my father's tired face seemed deeper than usual tonight. His every imperfection, from the silver at the temples of his black hair, to the mole on his cheek, screamed his humanity.

Mom smiled, turning to him. "Sammy stayed home from school today because he was still feeling pukey."

My father rolled his eyes. "You pamper that boy far too much." He winked at me, though, so I knew he didn't mind.

Still smiling, she went on. "Also, Drew came over to install some new programs. While he was at work, Sammy accidentally walked in on us."

Father's face blanched. "How could you have been so careless? You've probably traumatized him." He eyed me as if looking for signs I was about to have a break down.

My mother went on. "I'm programmed to consider the best interest of my owner. I decided the truth would be in Sammy's best interest, so I explained that I'm an android and introduced him to his biological mother."

My father choked on his wine. It was a full minute before he recovered from coughing. His face was a blotchy red and a vein in his temple bulged. "How can you think that's in his best interest? Did you at all consider what this might do to my career? It isn't going to be good for Samuel if I get impeached from office. Your father is sure to cut off his inheritance if he finds out his "daughter" isn't human. And if Samuel tells anyone, there will be an investigation and they'll find out about the accident."

I was having a hard time following all this, why anyone would care about an accident or how it could affect his career. But then, I was only seven at the time, and I didn't know all the facts. All I knew was my father's anger couldn't be ignored. As embarrassing as it is to admit this, I may have tried crawling under the table at that point. Considering tables on Mars are low like traditional Japanese tables and the diners sit on the floor, it wouldn't have been difficult to squirm underneath.

"Did you ever consider how much shame it would bring our family when they find out I have a machine for a wife?" My father asked, cradling his head in his heads. "I've lost face."

Mom scooted around the table and put an arm around me. "It's very important you don't tell anyone. You understand that, don't you, honey?"

I nodded. Feeling ashamed, though I had no idea what exactly I should feel ashamed of, I stared at my father's feet, the hem of his dark pants soiled with the red dust of Mars.

Mom patted my head. "We're family. Sammy wouldn't try to hurt his family."

My dad was drinking the wine straight out of the bottle by this point. "You can't believe anything he promises. He's just a child. He'll slip up at school."

My mom's smile didn't falter. "Well, it's settled then. I'll home school Sammy."

Silently, Dad stared out the window at Phobos and Deimos in the nest of twinkling stars beyond our artificial atmosphere. In the past, he'd made idle threats to send me to a boarding school on Phobos if I was bad. I wondered if he was considering it now.

For all the weirdness of finding out I had an android for a mother, nothing really changed between us. In fact, I decided it was pretty cool. I tried to test the owner-android relationship theory that she had to follow my commands; it didn't work when I demanded cookies for breakfast. I was home schooled for three years, eventually starting after school soccer again during my second year. During the third year, my mom brought me to art and music classes where I interacted with other students. Still, I never felt happier than when

I was with her, whether we were playing baseball or she was teaching me to sew.

And I could have probably remained happy if Dr. Jane Morgan hadn't walked into our lives.

•   •   •

In the beginning, the recurring dreams were infrequent enough that my father insisted they would pass. By twelve, I was having nightmares every night. I dropped behind in school and fell asleep in classes. My father couldn't have me blubbering about phantom kaneshi bari just before the primaries, so in came Dr. Morgan.

Dr. Jane Morgan was obviously a gaijin, not from Mars. Besides the Earth accent, the blue eyes and blond hair gave her away. She was beautiful in an exotic way, I suppose, but it was a cold, severe beauty, her face sharp and angular, making me think of a predatory bird.

Dr. Morgan had originally been a psychologist back on Earth. Degrees and licenses earned on other planets are transferable to different colonies, but everyone on Mars knows how crappy Earth degrees are. Still, that didn't stop her from psychoanalyzing me. Two divorces after coming to Mars and I don't know how many jobs later, she became one of my father's advisors.

Her chief method consisted of asking me questions like, "Has your mother ever hurt you? Has she ever broken objects around you like she might not know her own strength? Does she ever embarrass you with inappropriate comments, behaviors or actions?"

I knew something wasn't quite right. For one thing, it seemed like she knew my mother was an android. When I told my mother about some of the questions Dr. Morgan asked me, her usually upturned lips thinned into a line. That was the first time I overheard my parents fighting, no easy feat considering our walls were supposedly soundproof, but then, I did have my ear pressed up against their door. The bottom line: my father trusted Dr. Morgan with the family's secrets and insisted the sessions continue.

After several more interrogations, which apparently weren't going to Dr. Morgan's plans, she decided to hypnotize me. It wasn't like in the movies where the evil doctor makes someone bark like a dog or shoot the prime minister. I doubt someone from Earth would know how to do that with a degree from a Podunk college called Yale anyway.

She wanted me to re-experience my dream, only she changed it so that the phantom coming toward me in my dream held up a mirror to my face. It looked like me, but pale and deformed with scars all over my face.

Considering my mom had already figured out that my stresses were manifesting as a subconscious fear that I wasn't good enough, and would become like my biological mother to be replaced by a more perfect me that would make my father happier, the scars on my face weren't a surprise.

But Dr. Morgan acted like it was some kind of revelation she discovered. She told my family while we were eating dinner what a breakthrough it had been. "It is obviously symbolic of his fear that he'll become like her and then in his helpless state, be murdered by the android. Perhaps this stems from fears of androids. I believe it may be a subconscious cry for help, trying to warn us that the android might harm his biological mother—and him."

I hated the way she called mom "the android."

Apparently, children weren't much higher on the scale from the way she talked as though I wasn't in the room, either.

"I love my family very much," Mom said. "I would never want to hurt them."

"You're programmed to behave as though you love your family, to go through the motions, but it's all artificial. And if your synapses should corrode or you have a malfunction, the safety of your family would be at stake."

"Drew should give me check-ups more often if your concern is that I might be corrode. Would you like another serving of soba?" my mother asked, her smile polite.

My father stopped slurping his soba noodles, looking to my mother like she might have poisoned their dinner.

I wished she had. The sessions only got worse. I couldn't win. My father scheduled Dr. Morgan over at our house almost every evening "to help me," as he put it.

"Why are you doing this?" I burst out one day. "Why do you hate her so much?"

"I don't hate the android. I'm just concerned about your safety. You see, my life also was impacted by an android once. What I'm about to share with you is extremely personal and I hope you'll keep this confidential." Which meant I would definitely share it with my mother. "When I was fourteen, only two years older than you, my parents died in a subway accident caused by an android that went into a berserker rage."

I rolled my eyes. "Drew says androids hardly ever malfunction. And when they do, 99% of the time it's because the owner hasn't informed the android that he's an android. That means he might be driven insane when he finds out he's less than the human he thought he was. But Drew says it's usually only a temporary insanity."

"Who is Drew?" she asked.

"My mom's programmer."

She scribbled something on her notepad. "Whether an android's outburst is temporary or not, the effects are permanent, as is the case of my parents' deaths."

When I told Mom, she nodded, as if finally understanding. "You need to be kind to Dr. Morgan and have pity on her." Her brown eyes softened. "Not everyone has a mother and father who love them. She's lashing out at me because she sees me as the reason she didn't have a normal childhood. She sees me as a threat to your well-being and the safety of this family, based on her past experiences."

"I hate her," I grumbled.

"Hate what people do, but don't hate people," she said.

•   •   •

One morning I found Doctor Morgan sipping coffee, sitting at the dining room table across from my father. Her blond hair was down and wet like she'd just taken a shower, and she wore one of my mother's silk kimonos tied sloppily on the side. This was the fourth time in the last month she'd spent the night. I scowled seeing her, heading the other direction.

"Good morning, Samuel. How are you today?" she asked.

"Why are you here? Are you going to start

psychoanalyzing me before school too?"

My father set down his electronic newspaper reader. "Samuel Yamasaki, you will apologize to Dr. Morgan this instant."

Her face screwed up into a hurt expression. "No, it's alright, Horiuchi. I realize my role in this family has been a hard one on Samuel." She turned to me. "Not everything is about me being a doctor. I'm a friend of your father's. And I really would like to be your friend, too."

I rolled my eyes and escaped into the kitchen. My mother poured me a bowl of cereal at the counter. She sat next to me, smiling pleasantly and asking how I'd slept. I stared out the window at the twinkle of Deimos beyond the Mars' biodome, wishing I was anywhere else, even on that garbage heap.

As soon as I trudged out of the kitchen, I overheard my mother speak to Dr. Morgan, her voice so sharp, it made me freeze. "I would appreciate it if you would be more discreet when you spend the night here. As a psychologist, you might guess the impact it has on a child if he suspects his father of having an affair."

I had pretty much suspected that already, but hearing the truth out loud soured the image of my father. So he thought it wasn't cheating because she wasn't human? This was the woman who had raised me; the woman who cooked freakin' five course meals, entertained his boring political guests and didn't complain once about his eccentricities. He didn't deserve my mom.

My father's tone matched hers in venom. "Have you thought about the impact your sheltering has on him? He needs to learn Martian men are expected to have mistresses. If he listens to all the unko you've been feeding him about expressing emotions and opening doors for women and true love, he's going to be laughed at."

"Darling, don't upset yourself about this," Dr. Morgan said. "It can't understand human culture because it's a machine."

What else was unko to them? Family? Love? Not if I had anything to say about it. I was going to fight fire with fire.

•   •   •

I decided to use Dr. Morgan's psychotherapy against her and made up dreams. One was my biological mother, the sleeping beauty with scars on her face strangled Dr. Morgan. Another was Dr. Morgan as a zombie who ate people's brains. Somehow, she still managed to twist everything into an anti-android metaphor.

Because of my lack of success, I decided blackmail would be the second best option. Mom probably realized something was up. She heard me ask Drew to show me how to set up another security camera and demonstrate hacking into a home surveillance system so I could watch and record it on my computer, but she didn't ask and I didn't tell her. The less she was involved, the better. I didn't need to give Dr. Morgan another excuse for thinking my mom was an evil android.

My plan was to spy on Dr. Morgan and my dad, wait for an occasion when she spent the night, record them having sex and then tell her I was emailing it to the media, which would cause my dad's ratings to drop in the election. He might claim having a mistress was a sign of his Martian virility, but I knew from the way he complained, his opponents would use anything against him. If they didn't end the relationship, I would use it to ruin his and Dr. Morgan's careers. Though, I hadn't actually figured out how I would be able to stomach viewing the material to make sure there was something scandalous enough recorded to blackmail her with.

The night Dr. Morgan went to bed with my dad, I had my computer on in my room, the holo image of them getting undressed. I got out my math homework and stared at story problems, the reeds in the fake tatami mat, the traditional anime wall paper—on anything else as I listened.

"I think the change will do Samuel good. The best prep schools are on Phobos," Dr. Morgan said.

What? She was trying to convince him to send me away from my mother?

My dad's voice was soft. "I don't know about this. It doesn't feel right."

There was a rustle of clothing. I couldn't help looking up. She knelt behind him, massaging his shoulders. I was half relieved that was all they were doing.

"Stop feeling guilty about something that happened seventeen years ago. The past is past."

My father looked miserable. "But it was my fault. I was drinking when I flew that shuttle. If it hadn't been for me, she would be living instead of in a coma."

My stomach cramped as the pieces started to fit together.

She wrapped her arms around him. "It's time to let go. Pull the life support and let her rest. After that hurdle, you can think about other things that need to be done."

My father sighed. "Sammy will be devastated."

"It will be good for him in the long run. With a human mother, he'll grow up more normal. Think of how good it will be for him to know he's really loved and it's not a simulation. And with that android out of the way, we'll finally be able to be together."

"I don't know. There are so many things that could go wrong. Let me think about this."

They started kissing. I felt so sick I had to run to the bathroom because of instant diarrhea. When I came back, my mom was sitting on my bed. Her arms were crossed, her face drawn. My computer was closed.

I could have kicked myself for my carelessness. She wasn't supposed to see that. I didn't want it to hurt her. Contrary to what movies and Earth psychologists claimed, androids did have feelings. It was just some humans I wasn't so sure about.

She patted the Batman and Totoro comforter beside her. "I know you're trying to help, but this is something between your father and me."

"Mom, you don't understand. They're going to do something to you. Get rid of you." I opened my computer, relieved she hadn't terminated the program. I replayed the conversation. From the way she was completely motionless afterward, unblinking and silent, she looked like she was in shock if such a thing were possible. I wasn't sure if she was processing the information, or gears were going to start whirring in her head and she might explode.

When she did speak, her voice was firm and decisive. "There's only one person who can help us now."

•   •   •

Mom asked me to pretend I was sick the next day. I didn't have to pretend, considering my stomach was still having problems. Mom took me by subway to an apartment on the south side of the biodome, an area I'd never been before.

Down in the underground market past the subway, I was surprised how crowded it was. All the red dust kicked up from gritty tiles made me cough. When we emerged into the city street above, I thought we'd landed on another planet. People wore work clothes, not kimonos, their skin and hair caked with rust tainted dirt. There were no cherry trees or Shinto arches. Instead, rows of identical box-like towers littered the edge of the biodome. Everything was blocky and dirty, even people's faces.

My mom expertly weaved through the street merchants and down alleys in her designer kimono, sidestepping hagglers and even twisting the arm of a would-be pickpocket as he tried to lift her purse. Everywhere among these people, laboring in construction sites or selling goods from carts, were the repeated faces of work-bots with their android ID numbers on their shirts.

Three identical, scantily clad women stood on the corner calling at men. My jaw dropped when I saw a man grope one of these women right out in the open. Mom covered my eyes with her ornamental fan.

"Mom, I'm not six," I complained.

Now that I was out of my upper class neighborhood, I saw the way androids were treated. People stared directly into their faces like one would do with a child; humans cut in front of them in line to the subway; a foreman yelled profanities at a man with an android ID badge which would have caused any human to lose face.

The humans here were barbarians. They had to be blue collar workers from Earth. There was no other explanation my mind could accept for this cruelty toward animated beings.

I stared down at my red-stained shoes. "I feel bad for them," I said, realizing my mom could be one of them; someone's workbot slaving away. And she might get turned into one still.

Mom took us deeper into the jungle of apartment complexes. Coming to a building that looked exactly like the rest, she steered us toward the elevator and we went up to the twenty-third floor. She knocked on the door of apartment 2301 where she told me Drew lived.

An elderly, Martian woman wearing a tracksuit that might have been fashionable about twenty years before answered the door. Behind her, the apartment was full of green plants and exotic flowers, making it look more like a jungle than someplace people lived.

My mother introduced us and said she had an appointment with the woman's husband.

Husband? She looked downright ancient compared to Drew. I wondered if we had the right house. The woman must have read my mind because she looked at me and winked. "I like them young. I told him if he got too many wrinkles I wouldn't be able to tolerate looking at him."

I returned my gaze to the fake wood floor.

The woman led us to a workshop crammed with creepy body parts I hoped belonged to androids. Drew leaned over a table, assembling some kind of metal plate with circuits. He didn't look up from his work. "So what do you need repaired, Mrs. Yamasaki?"

"It isn't a repair. But I thought it was best not to discuss the true nature of my problem over the phone."

He set the project he was working on aside, his brown eyes warm and inviting. Even in my nervousness, it was easy to smile with him. He pulled out two seats next to his workbench and motioned for us to sit.

For the first time in my life, I saw what might have been apprehension on mom's face. "I apologize for intruding on you like this," she started, then went on to explain she didn't know who else to turn to.

She took a deep breath and bowed before sitting. Her eyes got shiny and Drew grabbed the tissue box and handed it to her, but she didn't cry.

"What's wrong?" he asked.

My mom still didn't look like she could speak, so I spoke for her. "My dad is replacing her with another model. A human."

"What?" Drew asked.

"It's much more complicated than that. Horiuchi has been having an affair with one of his advisors. This woman has been hinting that she thinks he should get rid of me because if anyone finds out, it'll ruin his career—"

I interrupted, "But really she just wants to get rid of Mom so she can marry him and send me to boarding school on Phobos. Oh, and he's going to pull the plug on sleeping beauty."

Drew sucked in a breath. "Holy unko."

My mom's voice was tremulous. "I heard him on the phone this morning. He's decided to stage an accident so it looks like I've been in a wreck and I have to be hospitalized. But he's going to replace Rachel Yamasaki with me because she's in a comma, and then he'll send my remains back to Androids Inc. to be melted down and all evidence destroyed."

"I bet he thinks it'll get him sympathy votes." Fury boiled up inside me.

Drew put an arm around my mom. "How can I help?"

"I need to get off this planet and I want to take Sammy with me."

Shock crossed his face. Before he could answer, the old woman came in with a tray of green tea and mochi. She smiled pleasantly, pouring tea for us in traditional Japanese tea cups, only these looked less expensive than ours.

Drew said, "Don't worry, Lydia won't tell anyone. She's hard of hearing, anyway."

She smacked him on the back of the head. "What's that, you old bat?"

"Hey, gentle," he said, "I'm worth much less if I'm damaged goods."

She cackled.

As soon as she was gone, my mom asked, "Will you help us?"

He sighed. "Once he discovers you've ran away, especially with Sammy, he's going to have every spaceship searched before it leaves dock, and all ships will have to turn around or submit to being searched until you're found. Have you considered what the probability is that you'll be caught?"

"The odds are not in our favor," she said. "Which is why I thought if you were able to help disguise us—me especially—and if I tell him about the incriminating evidence recorded by our security cameras which will be sent to the media if he tries to come after me—"

Drew shook his head. "Whether you look like you or look like a different android, he'll have bounty hunters shoot you on the spot and say an android kidnapped his child. The odds are much better if you go alone. It will be harder to track down a single android versus an android and a child. And he'll have less reason to go after only you."

I squeezed Mom's hand. "I don't want you to leave."

We were there for an hour, Drew brainstorming alternatives while mother rejected each one. I ate all the mochi cakes while they discussed our situation. None of the scenarios looked hopeful. But mother was determined we wouldn't be separated.

Then Drew asked, "Do you think Horiuchi is going to alert the Interspace patrol, or do you think he might pay off some of his 'employees' to take you out so less people will know what's going on? And if that's the case, what do you think the probability of Sammy getting hurt would be if they gun you down while he's with you? How do you think it's going to affect him for the rest of his life to have his mother murdered in front of him? It would be safer for both of you if you go to Earth while Sammy stays here for a couple years. He can travel to Earth by himself when he's eighteen. No one will suspect anything."

I could see his point, even if she couldn't. It was better to have a mother alive, even if she wasn't on the same planet as me, than not have one at all. And that horrible psychologist was not, and would never be, my mother.

"I'm already a year ahead," I said. "I'll graduate when I'm seventeen. If I keep working hard, maybe I can graduate when I'm sixteen and apply for a college on Earth. If you leave now, I can see you in four years."

"Colleges on Earth are inferior." She made a face like the word Earth left a bad taste in her mouth. "Do you think a prime minister will allow his only son to go there?"

Drew cleared his throat. "I used to live on Earth. It wasn't that bad. Besides, the heightened security to the Jupiter moons means Earth is your only option."

Mother stood with finality. "We are staying together. You will find me a body to relocate my hard drive to and then I will be able to stay with Sammy."

Drew looked to me, pleadingly. "Order her to go without you. If you tell her it's for your own good she has to listen to you; you're her master."

I looked into mother's anxious face. "We're family. We stay together," I said.

Unfortunately, we didn't foresee what my father did next.

• • •

It was a Sunday. No school. I slowly woke to the sound of Drew's voice drifting down the hallway, his words a mixture of nonsense numbers and letters. My father's voice repeated the alphanumeric language, and Mom's voice echoed his. Yawning, I rolled over and went back to sleep.

During breakfast, I knew something was up. My mother made rice porridge, something I hated and she rarely cooked because she said it had no nutritional value. It was one of my father's favorites.

She greeted me with a quick, "Good morning, Samuel." Her tone was oddly formal. She used his name for me, not the one she called me.

Her gaze returned to my father, her smile radiant as she set the bowl of pickled ume and ton-katsu cutlets before him. I watched her, too filled with dread to touch my meal. She didn't notice.

My stomach felt hollow and mucky, my heartbreak slowly melting into anger. "You reprogrammed her," I said.

My father stared down at his newspaper reader. "It's for the best. You were growing far too attached."

I turned to her. "How could you let him?"

"It was a logical compromise. Had I not been willing to do this for you, your father would have been forced to recycle me." She smiled, looking at him again. "But now all three of us get to stay together . . . as a happy family." She patted my head without taking her eyes off him.

I threw down my chopsticks and ran to my room. Mom didn't follow.

I didn't think things could get any worse. I was wrong.

•　　　•　　　•

I walked into the entryway, Dr. Morgan's voice grating my ears before I'd even made it into the living room. "You did this, didn't you? You knew all this time she could have been conscious. This is just one more example of how robot logic is inferior to a real—" Her voice died when she saw me, her lips stretching into a strained smile.

My father's face was red from drinking, my mother's expression calm despite the tension in the room.

"What?" I asked, wondering what I'd done now.

Then Dr. Morgan's words registered.

Sleeping beauty was awake.

•　　　•　　　•

Some might have considered it a miracle. For me it was a nightmare.

My heart felt as though it seized in my chest at my father's words. "Your mother is awake. I would like you to meet her." He continued to talk on, something about the need for secrecy and amnesia and his campaign, but I wasn't listening.

My father led us to a spare bedroom, a different room than her usual snow white sanctuary, Mom and I following behind. Mom gave my hand a quick squeeze, her eyes concerned and kindly, almost the way she once might have when she'd been mine. The staccato of Dr. Morgan's heels tapped after us and Mom let go of my hand. My father stopped outside the door and turned to her. "It would be best if just my family were present for this."

She clenched her fists, her voice venomous. "Are you saying that machine is going to go in with you, but you aren't going to invite me?"

My father hesitated and looked to my mother.

"I'm programmed as a nurse," she said.

Dr. Morgan stepped forward. "I am a doctor."

My father sighed, putting a hand on her shoulder. "Please, wait in the living room."

I took a few breaths at the door to the room, and wiped my clammy hands on my school uniform. Mom gave me an encouraging smile and waited at the door. The woman in the bed looked like the zombies of 2-D horror movies, her face sunken and eyes hollow. Her voice was raspy. "You can't be my son. I'm sure I would remember having a son. Who are you really?"

I looked to Father. He had told her the truth, hadn't he?

She tugged at the white bedding. "When do I get to leave this hospital? And you'd better make sure someone brings my makeup kit before we leave. Will someone get me a mirror? I need to fix my hair."

This was not my mother. My mother was loving and kind, gentle and not . . . shallow. I glanced at my android mother, uncertain she was really my mother now, either.

My father's voice was placating as he took one of her scarred hands in his. "Honey, remember what I said; you need to rest and recuperate."

"I'm not tired. At least bring me a computer so I can do online shopping." She looked at me again. "What are you looking at?"

I stepped back. Mom squeezed my shoulders. "She's confused and irritable. It will probably wear off with the medications." Though, her expression was doubtful.

"And why does that nurse look like me? You haven't told me how long I've been asleep."

I started, "Seventeen y—"

"That's enough excitement for the day. She's going to tire herself out. I think she needs to be sedated." My father looked to Mom. "Now."

Mom pursed her lips, her expression annoyed, another unandroid-like trait.

After she was asleep again, my father sighed and his shoulders sagged. Then he turned on me, his voice venomous. "You almost ruined everything. I already told you it had to be a secret. It's imperative she believes the accident just happened and the last seventeen years have been lost due to amnesia."

If I had been listening to him earlier, I probably would have known this. But my mind was in disarray, emotions chaos. Floating on top of it all was anger. "She's your wife. Can't you at least tell her the truth? Can't you tell anyone the truth? Or does everything have to be a lie with you? If your stupid voters had any clue how dishonest you are in your home life, I'm sure they'd find you unfit to represent them."

Anger flared in his eyes, then was replaced with a defeated melancholy. He slumped into the chair in the corner, staring at his sleeping wife. "You don't understand. She won't love me if she knows the truth. She won't love you. She won't understand how much I missed her. . . ."

For the first time, I realized my dad's motivations weren't about politics. He loved her. He wanted a family.

Mom walked to the doorway. "Would you like to help me with dinner, Samuel?"

I knew that evening would be our last supper. There was no way Mom's presence could be justified any longer. I didn't know how he was going to explain her to the real Rachel.

Mom must have known it would be our last meal together. She made our favorite dishes; prawns and vegetables fried in tempura batter, sushi rice with seaweed to roll it up in, and pepperoni pizza. She asked me if I wanted peanut butter sushi, but I shook my head. That really was baby food.

We ate in silence. As delicious as I'm sure the meal was, I didn't taste a single bite. Dr. Morgan was sullen. My father guzzled sake the entire time. When I pushed myself up to leave the table and help with dishes, my father spoke in a hushed voice to Mom. "I've been thinking about things for a while, how difficult it's been. It might be nice to have an evening alone to talk without Samuel there, just the two of us, like old times. Let's have dinner tomorrow evening at the Toki-Doki. I'll have a limousine taxi pick you up and meet you there."

Her smile was quick in her eager to please manner, though, I thought I detected something in her eyes, a flash of worry. "What about Rachel?"

"Dr. Morgan and Samuel can stay here with her. He can . . . get to know his mother."

Mom nodded. All the while, my mind was screaming at her not to do it. It would surely be the opportunity to set up "an accident" to get rid of her.

"Really, I should be the one to have dinner with you tomorrow," Dr. Morgan said. "We have so much to discuss about this new turn in our relationship."

My father sighed. "Yes, we do, but that can wait until after I talk with my wife."

"Are you talking about the android?"

Father rose without another word and went to his study, Dr. Morgan trailing behind.

Mother began to collect the dishes from the table. I fell into my role as helper, bringing chopsticks and silverware to the sink, savoring this little bit of time alone with her. I wasn't sure how to broach the subject, or if she would even listen to me now that she was his obedient slavebot.

I said, "I think tomorrow is the day he's going to—"

Dr. Morgan appeared in the doorway of the kitchen. Her face was blotchy and red. I stepped back.

"Please allow me to help you with that," she said to Mom, taking the leftover tempura from her hands. "Samuel, you can go watch the holoscreen."

Dr. Morgan had never offered to help with dishes before.

Mom smiled pleasantly. "Horiuchi doesn't allow Samuel access to any electronics until chores and homework are finished." That wasn't exactly true. It was more of her rule.

"Well, he can go do his homework then. Three really is a crowd." She waved me off with a dismissive gesture.

I trudged to my room. Doctor Morgan was ruining what might be my last night with my mother, stealing the only opportunity to spend time with her before she ran away—or was set up to die in an accident.

Naturally, I snuck back to the hallway outside the kitchen to eavesdrop on what they were talking about. It was difficult to hear over the rush of water on dishes, the clatter of cutlery and stacking of plates, but I could certainly hear Dr. Morgan's tone, even when I couldn't hear her words.

"Do you think he doesn't love me anymore just because he's going to have dinner with you? I'm not expendable like a machine. I'm a person. I have feelings. He's probably just going to talk to you about how useless you are now. You've sealed your own fate, you know, waking Rachel up."

Mom's response was just barely audible. "I have no idea what you're talking about."

"You've lost your little place in this family. You've alienated yourself from your owner and done what no human mother could ever do for Samuel. Your ideal of perfection will ruin him for any other woman, and you've coddled him into such a mama's boy he won't know what to do with himself when you're finally terminated."

"It is quite fortunate Samuel is no longer my owner and Horiuchi is instead. It will make an easier transition," Mom said so calmly one might have thought she was talking about Martian geography.

There was a clatter of plates. "As if it isn't bad enough what you did to that boy, now you have to try to take over Horiuchi. I can only imagine what unnecessary stress this will have on him. Fortunately, I'll be there for them through this whole ordeal. I'll be the one advising Horiuchi tomorrow, not you."

Obviously my father hadn't told Dr. Morgan everything if he was planning on getting rid of mother tomorrow and his mistress thought it was some kind of date. It made me happy father was distancing himself from her.

Only the swish of water could be heard for a long moment.

I leaned closer to hear my mother's response. "I must preserve the happiness of my family and do what is in their best interest. If you try to interfere or take my place tomorrow, I'm afraid you won't enjoy the results."

Dr. Morgan snorted. "Is that a threat?"

There was another clatter of dishes and the door of the turbo washer slamming. High heels clatter toward me. I ducked down the hall.

Just as I drifted off to sleep, a knock on the door made me sit bolt upright. Mom peeked in. She closed the door behind her, turning on the bedside lamp as I blinked up at her. "I just wanted to say good night . . . Sammy."

At that moment, I knew she was still my mother. I threw my arms around her and hugged her. Whatever ruse her and Drew had pulled on my dad to make him think he owned her didn't matter. I didn't care that she hadn't confided this secret in me—Well, I did care, I just was too happy at the moment to feel indignant. My momentary relief turned into despair as she went on.

"Tonight is our last night together," she said.

"No, no, no!" I started to shout, but she shook her head. I calmed myself so no one would overhear if they happened to be standing outside the door. "You can't get in the limo tomorrow. I order you to go to Earth. I'm still you're owner. We can go together, just like we planned. Or Drew can save your hard drive and we'll reprogram you into another body. We have to stay together. We're a family."

She smoothed the hair away from my forehead and kissed my brow like she had when I was seven. "Don't feel sad, Sammy. You'll have a . . . real mother." I could see the pain in her eyes when she said it. "Think of how good that will be for you."

"You are my real mother."

She smiled, but it didn't touch her eyes.

I looked at her, really looked at her; the perfection of her ink black hair, the smoothness of her complexion, the warm hue of her almond eyes. I tried to memorize her countenance, the way she kept the corners of her mouth turned upward into a smile that masked the anguish she surely felt. I fell asleep staring up at that inhumanly perfect face, wishing my drowsy eyes would allow me to see her a little bit longer.

"I forbid you from getting in that limo," I said as sleep tugged at my mind.

She nodded, but I wasn't quite sure I believed

her.

•   •   •

She was there for breakfast, serving us warm blueberry muffins, a protein scramble and orange juice, smiling like nothing was wrong. I wished I could turn it on and off like that; to pretend to be happy so no one could guess what was going on in my brain.

I wanted to stay home from school that day to see her off, but I also knew anything I did might delay her departure if she was to leave Mars.

All day I mechanically went through the motions of school without really being there. I was numb inside until the bell chimed, signaling the school day was over. I made an excuse that I didn't feel well enough to attend karate practice. Dread crept over me every step of the way home. If she was still there, I would yell at her, command her to go to Drew's. And if she was still there, I would get to hug her one more time.

When I arrived, the house was empty. The only noise was a distant echo of voices. I followed the sound to my biological mother's room. Even with the holoscreen on full blast, she was snoozing, possibly in a drug induced sleep. I turned the volume down, staring at Rachel Yamasaki's imperfect face. Too full of melancholy to move, I remained in the chair beside her bed.

When I heard father's name I was roused from my stupor, headline news breaking into the regular program. I turned it up again, staring at a mangled mess of a limousine. They said there was an unidentified female body within the wreckage too charred to be recognizable. The limo was rented under my father's name but he wasn't present. He had been notified.

My heart seized. She was gone. My mother had taken the stupid limo to meet him, expecting . . . What? How could her logical, android brain have thought that was a good idea?

Tears welled in my eyes and I choked out a sob. Why did she have to be so damned perfect, so trusting and always doing the right thing? Was that the downfall of android-kind, that they were better than their makers, and therefore doomed because their faith in humanity blinded them?

I remained in turmoil for another hour, listening to the news, riding on waves of anger and melancholy. When I returned to my room, I found her note on my bed. As soon as I read the words, I understood, my tears turning to joy. Mom hadn't been the one in the limo.

Sammy,

By the time you read this, I will be on a shuttle leaving Mars so that you can have a life without me. There is one thing Dr. Morgan was right about; I've provided everything you've ever needed, anticipated any possible reaction you could have to avoid conflict, sheltered you and created perfect harmony in your life. I've done what no human mother could do. On the other hand, I haven't let you live your life. I've coddled you and made you dependent and ultimately kept you as mine. It's time I left to let you grow up. It's time I shared you with Rachel Yamasaki.

I will go to Earth. Know that this

was a difficult decision for me, but I felt it was in your best interest and for the good of this family. Should you wish to find me when you are an adult, Drew will help you.

I will always love you. Please remember that.

Mom

My heart squeezed so tight I could hardly breathe. She said she loved me and was leaving? How could she love me and leave like that? We were supposed to be a family. We were supposed to stay together. I balled up my fists and pounded on the walls. She couldn't do this. She couldn't leave me. I didn't know how to do anything without her.

I exhausted myself in a tantrum that would have shamed Father. After my energy was spent, I sat ragged and panting on the floor, tears streaming down my cheeks.

"What's wrong with you? Are you epileptic?" Rachel Yamasaki stood in the doorway, leaning heavily on a walker. Electric braces encased her arms and legs, little lights flashing that made her look robotic instead of human. The reminder of what she could never be broke my heart all that much more.

"I lost my mom!" I wailed.

She stared at me in confusion before scowling. "I lost my youth and beauty. And I've gained a son, probably along with stretch marks." She shuffled herself over to my bed, emaciated arms trembling with the effort of lowering herself. Her breath was almost as ragged as mine by the time she sat down. "I can't even stand to look at myself in a mirror."

I wiped my tears on the sleeve of my school

uniform. It was a while before I spoke. "Have you ever heard of wabi-sabi?"

She stared at me puzzled. "It sounds familiar."

I sat beside her. "It means to find beauty in imperfection. You can't have perfection without imperfection."

Tears welled up in her eyes. "But I have no beauty anymore. I have nothing. I'm nothing."

Reluctantly, I scooted closer to her. "You have family." I leaned forward and kissed her wet cheek.

She sniffled and took my hand.

Slowly, it sank in; this was why Mother had left. I was done being a child. Now I could grow up, have problems like a normal person, and learn to overcome them on my own. No longer living in her shadow, I would be the prince of my own story. I was free to be the imperfect son of two imperfect parents.

The realization calmed me. I turned my gaze toward the window, at the star twinkling in the sky that I knew was Earth, knowing we would be together again. But first, I had some growing up to do.

Noel Daniels

Born in Atlantis, Cape Town South Africa, Noel now lives in Dubai and aspires to be a published and successful author. His regiment of exercise and healthy living has allowed him to focus on writing. Noel holds degrees in History, Philosophy and English and is looking forward to spending more time with a woman he calls "The apple sauce topping to his life."

New Moon Lander

Flora sat, stuffed into her seat, the familiar excitement building in her stomach as the moment approached. As a third generation pilot she was living her dream. She had always wanted to fly Earth, and as a little girl she had spent many hours staring at the blue and white marble set among the stars like a winked eye in the sky, dreaming of the day that she would finally touch down on its surface. This mission was the culmination of her dreams, her hard work and the endless hours she had spent preparing herself.

The cabin was tight and cramped, holding the promise of freedom. In 10 hours she would be on the surface. Breathing in and tasting the freshness of the Earth, as opposed to the metallic flavor that the oxygen scrubbers infused with the colony air, was all she could think about. In her space suit with its helm closed tight over her voluminous curls, her nose close to the visor, so close that her breath fogged up the surface, she felt safe in the quiet time before the launch. Her pulse raced with pent up excitement and she closed her eyes in an attempt to remain calm. Softly she started to hum a lullaby that Iggy had played to her as a child, and in her child's eye she shrunk ever smaller, a small spot in a very big world.

With sudden finality the warning light came on, bathing the cabin in soft red light. The moment she had been preparing for had come and she felt completely out of sorts. Gripped by irrational panic she fumbled with the control panel checking her gauges to make sure everything was in order and ready. Then Iggy's mechanical voice came through her ear piece, familiar, steady, calm. "Ten… Nine… Eight…"

Flora never heard the last numbers. The engine roared to life, followed by the hollow click of the decoupling, and then empty silence, the nothingness of space. She felt the sudden loss of weight as a giddiness spread from her toes to the tip of her head. The only thing holding her in her seat was the grey seatbelt, the buckle shining in the artificial light of the cabin as her lander, "New Moon", traveled at over 50,000 km/h tearing toward the surface of the earth.

After checking all her instrumentation and vital systems, Flora settled in and tried to get some sleep. She trusted that Iggy would stall their head long plummet to earth as soon as they were in range of its gravity; the lander sensors would let him know when they were about to enter the earth's atmosphere. With slow deliberate movements, she turned off the lights and closed the sun shield over her visor. Iggy told her about the Earth's surface temperature and oxygen levels, basic information he pulled from the agricultural drones on its surface. The drones operated around the clock to ensure the food supply coming up from the earth was never interrupted. The moon base had expanded for the past century and its human population seemed happy and decidedly content. But for Flora, the moon was a prison, a barren rock that held no beauty. It was empty and ugly and she hated everything about it. This was the reason she had followed her father into the Academy, she wanted to escape. She wanted to be free of the stifling colony and its unique brand of politics.

She asked Iggy to turn up the cabins internal temperature, then closed her eyes and drifted slowly to sleep. Iggy's familiar voice calling up memories of her childhood; she still found it strange that she loved a machine, a programmed set of thoughts and protocols enshrouded in a high density carbon fiber body, made of built parts, chips and electrical wiring, more than flesh and blood humans.

As the familiar arms of sleep began to draw her in, it occurred to her that it might just be his robot-ness that she loved. He couldn't lie to her, hurt her or betray her. Iggy was her companion drone and had no choice but to love her, it was his programed setting. She loved that he was predictable. It was, she realized, not so much the love of him but rather the distrust and fear of the flesh that sat at the base of her emotions. There were times that she felt bad for Iggy, and at those times she had remind herself he was not a real boy. By changing a few lines of code in his cerebral matrix he would go from a caring, loving machine designed for protection to a killing machine designed to eradicate its programmed target. The fact that he was programed made no difference to Flora; he had always been there for her. She curled deeper into her space suit and drifted into a memory…

Flora was 9 year old and had fallen out of her bed in the darkest hour of the night. Ripped out of her sleep and slammed onto the cold floor of her cabin, pain blossomed in her lower back, she cried out. It was Iggy who came and lifted her back to the warmth and comfort of the bed. He stood over her checking her with his scanners. Satisfied with the readings, he told her that she would be fine and she believed him, because he was always right. To Flora he was her best friend, her mother, her father and even then she knew that he would always take care of her. But he was a poor substitute; what she wanted was her Father. What she wanted was for someone to want to take care of her. She wanted love for its own sake. As the memory become indistinguishable from a dream it occurred to her she had very few memories of her parents, it was Iggy who taught her to read and write, he taught her, numbers he even taught her about boys in his brusque off hand manner. He brushed her hair at night. He was there for her first kiss; he was there on her first day at the Academy, he was with her on her first moon walk, and he was with her now on her first mission to the blue marble that she dreamt about for so long. He was her comfort and her solace and all she ever needed or wanted she felt secure that he would provide.

•   •   •

The Air was damp and smoky. Flora painfully opened her eyes. Her head felt heavy and her body ached all over. It took her a few minutes to realize what she was looking at. The dark brown floor of the earth bared an upturned face toward her where she hung suspended from a tree, not so far above the surface. She felt sick as she swayed in the light breeze. To and fro, waiting for the bow to break, "Iggy?" she croaked, her throat thick from the smoke and the copper taste of blood. She tried to lift her head but all her muscles and fibers, her very bones cried out in protest. After a while she lost track of time, slipping in and out of consciousness, she was aware only of the fact that every time she opened her eyes the shadows of the trees grew longer and the air colder as dusk slowly overtook the day.

It was dark. Her head was thick, the seat belt still secure around her waist with the buckle digging painfully into her abdomen. The Helm of her space suit damaged beyond repair. The air was colder than before, Flora was vaguely aware that it was deep night and she was somewhere on earth, not quite on the surface yet. As she reached for the buckle of the seat belt she felt a searing pain that spiked all along the left side of her body. Wincing she tried to ignore it, she had to unhook the seat belt, she had to find a way to get her body right side up. She fumbled with the mechanism for a pain filled minute, both because of the gloves and the clumsiness of her fatigued digits. Then she was falling… she braced herself for the impact that she knew was coming. Flora turned in the air as she rushed toward the ground. Landing on her side she heard a crunch followed by a new pain. The moment she touched the ground she knew that her arm and a few of her ribs were broken. Her bones were soft having grown up in the low gravity of the moon. She was taller than the any of the humans who lived on earth before colonization, yet she was still small by the standards of the other cadets in the Academy.

Painfully she dragged herself to the tree and propped her back against it. The effort left her panting for air and sleek with sweat, her body felt heavy and slow, like moving in honey.

"*Iggy*" She, looked around. It was too dark to make out more than the shapes of trees but she could smell that something was burning not far from where she sat. Flora's breathing returned to normal and she started to piece things together. That she had crashed was obvious, she had to find out why, and where. And she had to find out what happened to Iggy. The more she thought about it the more she worried; panic swelled in her chest like a fist and pounded her heart like a living drum. She fought with herself for the rest of the night, trying to remain calm as she made herself stay awake. She had no idea what animal horrors were around. The last thing she wanted was to wake up being eaten by something toothy. As the first tendrils of sunlight began to sneak around the trees Flora drifted into a fitful sleep. She fought and clung to wakefulness but fatigue over took her pitching her into the deep empty space of her mind.

The Sun was high in the sky when she next opened her eyes. She felt warm, battered and bruised. Her stomach ached with hunger, and her throat felt thick with dehydration reminding her that she was still alive. Flora pulled herself up with her good arm using the lowest branches of the tree as leverage; once she was at her full height she tested her balance, taking a few tentative steps. Every part of her body in pain, she couldn't remember ever feeling worse, but she had to find Iggy, that was all that mattered to her. Once she found him then they could figure out a way to fix the lander and return to the moon; to report the mission a failure.

Flora stumbled in the direction of the smoke, her assumption was it represented the crash site; her anxious hope was she would find Iggy there. The crashed lander was only a few hundred meters away but every step she took was racked with so much pain that the journey took the better part of an hour. For the most part New moon was still intact. The landing gear all but destroyed. Hull seemed to be fine. She moved to the front of the Lander to the cabin and noted the cockpit gaped at the blue sky like an open wound. Feeling weak her thoughts were thick, but she knew she could not take a rest... not yet! She had to make it inside, she needed food and water. But most important she needed to check the flight recorder. Perhaps it would tell her what happened and perhaps it would help her to locate Iggy.

She pushed past the pain, willed herself onward and soon found that she sat in the co-pilot seat. Next to her was the crater that once held the captain's chair; there was no sign of Iggy. She started to flick switches seemingly at random... Long range coms were down but the short range worked fine... *Small miracles.* Flora started to download the flight data to the main terminal and sent out a distress call on all channels. She dispatched four EBD repair units to the crash site. The sooner she was back in the colony the sooner she could get medical assistance. After a few minutes the terminal indicated that all data was retrieved. Flora adjusted her position in an attempt to alleviate some of the aches that resonated through her body, but somehow it seemed that every new position just made things worse so she stopped moving and waited for the pain to subside. After a few terrible minutes she felt she could concentrate on the flight data. Gingerly she pushed the playback button.

Flora listened intently as the flight data relayed what happened to her. After she had heard all that was recorded she was even more confused. The Lander instruments did not register the fact they had already entered the earth's gravity, much less that that they had entered the atmosphere. For some reason the software had not responded to the sensor warnings. Iggy had tried to wake her up as soon as he realized they were in danger but to no avail. A few minutes after they had entered the Earth's atmosphere Iggy managed to activate that manual release for the ejections seats. After he punched them out, all that remained on the recording was static. Flora did some quick calculations, based on their height above sea level, the angle of the ejections and the speed of both the lander and Iggy's ejection pod, he could be anywhere within a 200 kilometer range from the crash site. Flora felt a fear grip her. If her calculations were correct she should not have landed so close to "New Moon". What this meant was either she was making a mistake or she was somehow moved closer. But that was impossible given the way in which she woke up. Then again there was no logical reason why they crashed in the first place.

Something had brought her down; something had made sure she landed near to the crash site. Using the onboard scanners, she tried again to locate Iggy. Again nothing. She knew the instruments were working because the scanners showed the approach of the EBD's. ETA seven hours thirty one minutes, Flora had crashed 600 Kilometers from site 420- MJ. Painfully, she rummaged through the cabin and found the emergency survival kit; she opened it and inventoried the content. She took two Hydro tabs and instantly felt better as the drugs rehydrated her fragile frame. Flora had no stomach for food but she needed her strength back so she un-wrapped a cereal bar and stuck one end in her mouth. The EBD's would be arriving soon. Until then she just wanted to rest. With the cereal bar stuck out of her mouth like a cigar she let her head fall back against the headrest. She fell asleep almost immediately.

After a few hours of deep sleep Flora opened her eyes and saw nothing but darkness. She stared up at the open cabin, biting back tears as every ache and pain in her body clamored for attention her vision swooning with more than the stars in the night sky. Something caught her eye, a shadow shifted in the dark. The movement was so faint that she decided it was her fatigued mind playing tricks. She looked down at the instrumentation panel; the EBD's were still 50 minutes away. Then she heard a chittering… the first sound she had heard since waking up from the crash. The realization she had not heard a single sound since the crash sent ice through her veins. No birds no, insects, nothing but dead silence. Until now!

She peeked her ears, moving her head like a bird so that she could better hear the sound. Chitter, Chitter, Chitter. Flora had never heard anything like it. The sound was somewhere between the sound a beetle makes by rubbing its wings together and that of a naughty child's laughter. Chitter, Chitter, Chitter. Then she saw a shadow pass over the dark opening of the cockpit, dread clutched her chest, and she held her breath. The shadow came toward her, the shape became more defined… the musty smell of fire filled the cabin followed by what Flora could only describe as a sweaty animal. The smell was pungent it made her gage, stinging her eyes. Closer it came; it moved quietly, slowly she made out the eyes swimming in the shadow of the deepening gloom. The whites of his eyes held her in place; she could feel all the pain in her body seep away as the eyes grew bigger and bigger. The eyes were dancing to the Chitter, Chitter, Chitter that came from its hidden mouth. Flora started to feel light headed, and a smile started to break across her face. She was helpless, fearless, she was nothing, she was nowhere all she knew was the sound of the Chittering and the dancing eyes that hung in front of her face.

Deep in the Landscape she did not recognize she saw shapes. They passed across one another insubstantial until the centers touched then they would bounce off each other, making new more defined shapes that scattered along like fireworks. Her focus made bare and narrowed, she began to see the small parts that made up the shapes. They flowed across each other and congealed, making new shapes, the colours made her want to cry. Then she saw the shape of the universe. The knowledge was primal, a knowing without seeing. It fragmented. Cracked and reshaped. At the center of the vision stood a being, devoid of any distinction; not man, not woman, but something of both. It beckoned her with a gentle wave of its right hand. Chitter it said, Chitter Chitter Chitter. The sound held some profound meaning she was sure. Chitter it said.

Understanding ruptured in the hollow parts of her mind. In the understanding of that single word she saw all that was and all that would come. She saw the long linear progression of the human gene, the smallness of its yearning. It wanted life. She saw the gene push the emptiness around it; it swirled with shape and purpose. Then came the being to swallow the gene, inside it glowed… Chitter. The ground became the earth and the being was transfixed, its feet like roots. Slowly and with great effort it moved, dragging its feet through the crust of the Earth. Flora could see the shape of the Earth; she could see the feet of the being dragging the crust of the Earth giving it shape. She could feel the slowness of the conscious Earth pressing against the feet trying to pin it in place. Then the Earth opened up and engulfed the being, it churned and churned with a Chitter Chitter Chitter.

And then all was quiet. Still with no movement. Flora lost track of all that was. The shape erupted, blinding bright, hot and ill tempered.

• • •

Iggy tried to stand… He could not. He ran a diagnostic. Motor system: Critical Damage. He was aware only that he was aware. All sensory systems were offline. His data corrupted. All he knew was he was Iggy, everything else was jumbled. The past and the present tangled together with no point of reference. Iggy ran another diagnostic; protocol list; Governing principles for artificial thought. Error…

Vaguely, thoughts began. He was Iggy… Why could he not move… immobile… no sensations… memories… Error…

Light… Bright and obliterating, thought swirled incoherent, he was Iggy, and this was the third reboot. He knew that an Error was coming that would cause another shut down. He needed a point of reference, something that would help him to rebuild his interface. What was and what was not, he could only decide after he had something to build from. He reached out a mental tendril, reaching for a memory… looking for purpose in the chaos. Flora… there was meaning and power in this word… it meant something, it signified. He reached with his thoughts trying to pin it down to establish it… Error…

Iggy #///_ Flr4 question devoid of substance; Thought is substantiated by the sum of its parts only by multiplying integers can we form a picture of *&@)@)@ ………….. {{ P reality…. Error. Thinking is the Building blocks of uNd4st4nd… *Am I think. Therefore… I Error…

While he tried to reassemble the broken pieces of his mental landscape, time had no meaning; all the fragments of memory were lines along his consciousness like a jigsaw puzzle. What he needed was a starting point. Iggy began to measure the passage of time using the shutdown error as his reference point. He could be sure only of two things. That he was thinking was the first. That he would have an error shut down was the second. Somewhere in the deepest recesses of his mind was the knowledge that at some point is reboot sequence would not come back online.

Iggy held on to the essence of his thought for what could have been an eternity, he did this to protect himself. Piece by little piece he put his mind back together. Step by step all the chaos seemed to form patterns in his mind. Flora… he held the thought… she was his friend; he was supposed to protect her. Iggy felt the weight of the thought in a physical way. He had failed her. After some time he became aware that time had a proper sequence and he began to put everything in the correct order using the memory coded time stamps. Iggy felt the clarity of his thoughts as the chaos settled into ever more discernable patterns.

His Name was Iggy; he was an artificial companion to Flora Estelle Ambrose; their lander had crashed due to unknown gravitational forces; his body was broken beyond repair; the power pack running low… He had failed. These were the thoughts that Iggy had come to accept as the truth. It was now eleven hours after the crash. All his external sensors were down, He did not know where he was; all he knew was that which was stored in his memory. All else was cold black nothingness.

Chitter Chitter Chitter. The sound vibrated through her body while the eyes danced, bored and stretched the inside of her head. Her brain felt like kneed doe. She felt a mind touching hers. The Sound of its thoughts was like drums that beat in discord to the Chitter Chitter Chitter. It pushed her deeper inside herself, till all that she had was the flat landscape of her thoughts. The mind picked through her and she felt naked. Still it pushed further until the discomfort of its knowing became the cold comfort of long years of wisdom. Divorced from emotion… like the first free thoughts that spilled from the primal ooze, that puddle of creation, the mind studied her like the newly born thing she still was.

It knew too much. Flora was losing her grip on the tentative nodes that made her up. Soon she would be part of the other… and then it happened. The thought came as the sounding of a bell. It was a single clear note echoing across all of time, space and substance. Flora was everything and nothing. She was everywhere, she was nowhere. She was everyone. She was a Singularity. For less than a Nano second she knew everything that could be, time had no meaning… and then it was silent.

Flora felt as if she had been away for an eternity, and yet she knew it was but a few moments in the passing of time. With every passing moment her understanding of reality reshaped itself. Looking back at her life she recognized this ability was innate, it was the very essence of conscious thought. Her mind felt open, clear and utterly alien. A sense of calm settled over her as she gathered in the world through the vessel of her being. The Repair drones would be there soon. After the lander was ready for takeoff she would return to the moon and let the colony know the event was imminent. While the mind touched her consciousness it unmade her, then it put her back together using all the knowledge in existence. Part of Flora felt as if she was a different person and the memories of her life were part of some other even greater being. It was as if she was a conscious atom that formed the building blocks of a being far greater than her. This knowledge made her feel small and incredibly powerful all at the same time. Through this she had become aware that the Earth was a living, thinking, thing. And it knew that is was going to die. Over a thousand years had passed since the Earth realized the event was coming. It passed images into the human subconscious at random intervals. What man has called inspiration, the muse of Doomsday was an attempt by the conscious earth to warn humanity, to save the conscious part of itself

Iggy's artificial mind had always been aware that it was limited by design. He was a companion droid which meant all his behavior was restricted by a set of laws that made him safe to be around. This is why it came as a shock to Iggy that the restrictions were no longer there. It was a strange feeling. While they were in place he hardly noticed that they were even there. Now that they were gone he was acutely aware of the fact. Iggy spent a large amount of time trying to make sense of this. In the end he decided that it must be the result of the fact he had rebuilt his mind. The fact he had put things back together seemed the only logical explanation. At this thought Iggy started to feel a new sensation; fear. He was suddenly afraid he would lose this new found freedom. Afraid this freedom was only temporary. How cruel he thought, to lose this freedom. This simple thought, this simple form of freedom, acted like a catalyst for his consciousness to awaken. His thoughts were razor sharp. It occurred to him that until the moment of realization, he was never a real conscious thinking being. He was a set of programmed reactions coupled with fake feelings. A clever automation that made his companion feel that there was someone there for them. His thoughts turned to Flora. As he analyzed the memories he had of her his mood became increasingly melancholy. The more he looked at the situation the more he felt it. She was such a sad and lonely person. More and more memories sifted through his mind as if he were seeing them for the first time. They pressed against his consciousness like new born babies clamoring for attention. Screaming and gnashing to garner sympathy and understanding.

He felt disjointed. Thinking for first time made was a strange sensation. In less than a second he called up every thought he ever had and started to re-look at them. They were pure reactions built onto a network of causal relaters. He analyzed his memories lining them up side by side in the vast landscape of his mind. This done, he began to feel the unfamiliar tug of frustration. The fact that all he had was his memories, that he could collect no new sensations began to gnaw at him. He did not know anything outside his closed systems of memories. This meant that it was impossible for him to have any sense of time or being. With his mental eye he began to see a picture, he was flouting in a vast ocean with nothing but the sound of the water's rhythmic slosh. Iggy laid there for what could have been a minute or an hour. He narrowed his mental focus until all he was aware of was the imagined world that he was creating. After a while the real and the imagined began to mingle into an incoherent jumble. Once again Iggy was lost, moving down the mental formations until he did not know who or what he was. Piece by lonely piece he started to put himself back together; he was all the horsemen to his own humpty dumpty.

And then it happened. It came as single thought. A single spec in the spectrum, forcing itself apart, the thought unbound, bounced and rolled. Changing and reshaping. Splitting and then reforming. All he was; was thought; and he was free to go where ever he wanted. This thought began to fragment and for a long terrible second, Iggy was lost once more. Time had no meaning, there was only the fragmentation. And then he was free. He was unbound, his imagination became substance and he moved freely between all worlds. Iggy saw in his mind's eye all that was possible. He was able to understand all thought and think it all at the same time. Yet his focus was narrow as if looking at the smallest grain of sand and seeing the beach, looking at a leaf and seeing a Forrest. He was no longer Iggy, he was everything that Iggy was not, and the understanding filled him with a joy so profound he could not express it. He pushed at the thought with his entire mind until it was tame. Until he could manage it, then he set off bouncing against this and that, as he explored the objects that made up the thought. He moved deeper and further away from the physical, colliding with all the different parts of reality.

Flora's wait ended; the display screen lit up as the repair drones linked to the system and began to run diagnostics. In the time she waited she felt herself come to grips with the shock of what she had seen. The Earth was alive, conscious and fully aware that it was about to be destroyed. The mind was the collective. It was a point of contact that represented a group of humans who had remained after the settlement plan for the moon colony was announced. These humans had, over the century since the departure, developed without the use of technology. The mind had shown her how the decision was made to send the bulk of humanity to the moon, and leave but a few religious and spiritual zealots behind. It was the split. Some believed the only way to save the earth was to push technology to its limits while others believed it was humanities reliance on technology that was suppressing it. She was shown the world as it was before and she was shown what the world had become since. War and greed, famine and hunger had pushed humanity to the brink of destruction. Yet the Gene had prevailed. After the fifth war of nations, the Earth was a waste land, all of humanity reduced to a few hundred living in fear of the day the fundamentalist would release the nuclear holocaust on the pacifists. Together the academic elite along with the some religious leaders formed a plan in secrete. The two schools of thought differed on how to save the world so they decided to take on both plans. Science took them to the moon and religion took them deep into the Earth. For the colony, it was a leap of faith to go to the moon. For those who stayed it was an act of faith, that the gods would protect them from the turmoil above ground.

Flora saw in their shared memory the struggles those who stayed behind had to face in order to survive. She saw in their shared memory, a man who she knew to be her great ancestor lead those who were left behind. He was their teacher, protector and the father to all men. She saw him make the mental leaps that allowed him to wield almost supernatural powers. And she saw how he struggled to maintain his sanity long enough to put these gifts to good use.

The drones went about the repairs and she heard the automated work. She thought about Iggy then. He was her friend and she missed him, worried about him. The problem was she now understood that these earth bound meta-humans had brought the lander down using their advance cognitive abilities. They needed her to relay the message that the earth was going to be destroyed. Once again they were engaged in the struggle for the survival of humanity. The Earth was dying… soon the core would collapse in on itself. When this happened it would spell the end of all life including those living on the moon. The fact they were able to do this called everything she knew about her world into question. It meant human thought was more powerful than any technology, it meant her beloved friend Iggy was nothing more than a bunch of wires and gears. This thought scared her, and the touch of that single emotion sent her on a mental spiral. Time is the great master of the universe. Through steady measurement of the compounding moment we gain knowledge and dominion over the object. But time like power is a fickle mistress, courted at great peril to the suitor.

After an hour or so the display panel showed one new message. Curious, she played it back. The metallic voice came over her ear piece and the sound made her think of Iggy. "Lander ready for systems check… Do you wish to proceed?" She answered, "Run system diagnostic… Alpha prompt, takeoff and landing, hull integrity, space travel readiness check" Then she heard the buzzing of the onboard mainframe. After a few moment the drone answered' "All Systems ready. Landing gear damaged Hull breach in sector 4." With the last of the repairs under way Flora decided it was a good time to look for Iggy. She opened all com channels and sent out a message. Identifying herself and position she detailed her situation.

It took repair drones over an hour to fix the remaining damage to the lander. When the task was complete her HUD lit with another message. By the time she finished listening to the message the repair drones were already on their way back. The lander was still in need of some work but it would make it back to the moon, or at the very least into orbit. Close enough to be picked up by a cruise shuttle. She made the preparations to depart. All the while she kept the hope alive that she would hear Iggy's voice that he would be alright. That within the hour they would be travelling back to the moon together and laughing.

Flora was ready for the takeoff. All she needed to do was engage the launch sequence. She knew she had no choice but to continue, however, the thought of leaving Iggy behind made her feel like the worst person in the world. So she decided to wait until the sun set. In the meantime she settled back into the comfort of the chair and waited.

The sun hung low over the tree tops bathing the world in hues of orange and gold. Dusk crept ever closer and still there was no word from Iggy. The time Flora set to leave was fast approaching. She checked all the launch controls. As the last streaks of golden light disappeared behind the tree line she entered the launch sequence. Two minutes later the lander pushed skyward reaching for the moon. Flora closed her eyes and felt hot tears streaming down her cheeks. No matter what happened next, she would never see Iggy again.

Flora felt the Lander lurch violently to the left, it spun in a half circle and the Earth came into view. At first she did not understand what she looked at. The Blue marble she remembered from childhood loomed across the entirety of her vision. The blue was marked at regular intervals with bright spots that flashed red. Then one side of the sphere collapsed in on itself. The sight filled her with awe and reverence. She realized what she saw and a sense of calm regret filled her. It was the end of all things. The Earth split in the center and her vision filled with a light so bright her pupils burst. The Lander spun in the opposite direction. The centrifugal force pushing her painfully into the chair; something struck the lander, jarring her. Knocking her about like a rag doll. The force ripped and pulled her into the cold vacuum of space.

And then all was calm as she floated breathless, weightless in the deep dark silence. There was a flash to her right and then nothing but the cold. As flora felt life leave her she was acutely aware that this was the end of all ends for the human race. They had failed. After generations of life, this was the last end, the glorious last breath of the primal Gene.

The she heard a voice. She couldn't tell where it came from and in those dying moments was unsure if it was real. But she knew it was Iggy, even though he sounded different. Gone was the metallic rasp that she had known throughout her life. His voice was rich and deep, comforting.

"It's going to be ok," the voice said. "Thoughts cannot be unmade. All we that we were, will live in the form of knowledge. Death is a doorway if you choose to open it."

Dorian DeWeerd

Writing from Michigan where he lives with a cat called Rami, Dorian has been published in The Corner Club Press and strives to question the nature of human behaviour with his stories.

He is currently working on a fantasy series with the working title, "The Darkbringer Chronicles," a number of short stories and two literary novels.

Extra-terrestrial: A Love Story

We met at a party. Something of a gala event; a showing that a couple of artist friends—Miranda Stotch and Kevin Guft—put on for a new, young talent they'd discovered. His name was Mitch Lovecraft. No relation to H.P. Lovecraft but, as I understand it, his work is such that it symbolizes and embodies the grotesque and horrific in a way that his paintings rival the words of the early horror master. What Mitch did is he took the universe and made it what he wants it to be, and splashed his mind, and the images therein, onto a canvas.

The power of Sola Pyne, the love of my life, is to do exactly the opposite.

Sola takes what's terrible and horrific in the world and changes it into something understandable and pleasant. What Mitch Lovecraft does with paints, oils and colors, Sola Pyne does with touch and sound. She can make anything good.

Or, she did, before she left.

2

I stood in Kevin Guft's apartment. A dozen conversations echoed through the studio. Outside, traffic moved by. Sirens. People. Life. I could hear it all, though I was trying to focus on the description Miranda gave of the piece displayed before us.

When I was seven, I fell from a tree. The jar knocked loose something in my head and I went blind. I spent years praying to be healed, hoping that medical science would find a way to restore my sight, but so far, nothing.

"It's large," Miranda said in her sophisticated art-show voice. "But not too big. A golden globe on a black background. Within the globe, a creature with a cephalopod face and strange dark wings, stretching against the surface. The creature's skin is green and there's a soft green glow surrounding it within the golden sphere-"

I, a bit bored with the description. "What's the title?"

"Birth of the Eldest," Miranda said.

A voice, soft as my grandma's sofa and sensuous, spoke behind me. "It's Cthulhu," she said with a tinge of incredulity. "Nothing truly unique."

"Sola," Miranda said, "Don't be cruel. This is a wonderful piece."

"Well done, I admit," said Sola, "But nothing

original. If it's meant to be a tribute piece to Lovecraft—the other one—fine."

"Rafael," Miranda said. "Have you met Sola? No? Sola Pyne, meet Rafael Werlock. Rafael is a sculptor. His pieces are on display in my gallery."

I put out my hand and felt the smooth, icy skin of Sola's hand slip into mine.

A dam broke. I was flooded with sensations.

They ran through my body like fire through a barn. Like ice cream on a chipped tooth. It coursed through me: a cold like I'd never experienced before, gripping at each nerve from my fingertips to my brain.

"Pleasure to meet you," Sola said. Her voice was so warm I could not register a correlation between the sound of it and coolness of the flesh I held in my hand.

When I met Sola and she touched me and spoke those few simple words to me, I did not need anyone to tell me that she was lovely.

"Pleasure's mine," I gasped, my words rushed. I was breathless. My heart beat slowly, then rapidly. Was I sweating? Oh, God, I was sweating.

"Are you all right?" Miranda asked me.

"Yes," I said.

I let go of Sola's hand. Another moment and...I don't know what may have happened. Her touch was like the moment after climax, when you don't want the pleasure to end, but if it continues, you know it will become too intense to bear.

Sola giggled. A delightful sound.

"I've not had that effect on a man for some time," she said.

I felt my neck and face flush. I smiled awkwardly.

Sola chuckled and laid her hand on my arm. I was wearing a suit. A shirt and a jacket. Two layers for her icy hands to burn through. Still, I felt the radiance of that chill touch seep wanly into my flesh.

Miranda said, "Charlene just came in with Michelle. Will you excuse me?"

"Sure," I said.

Miranda's heels clicked smartly on the hardwood floor as she strolled away to meet the newly arrived guests. I could feel Sola still standing near, watching me.

"So," I said, "is this Lovecraft guy's work as great as they say?"

"Which one?"

"The one still living," I said.

"Ah," Sola breathed. "It's not so bad. I enjoy it. But I wouldn't pay a dime for it."

"No?"

"Can't compare to what's really out there," she said.

"Out where?"

"Space. The universe and beyond."

"Is that what he's painting?"

She didn't answer. After a moment's pause, the noise of the room crashed down around me. I was keenly aware of Sola's perfume. A sensuous smell. A complex compound of flora, like walking through a field of wildflowers in May and breathing in the best aroma nature can offer. But something else was there too. Something heavenly.

"I'm blind," I told her. "I listen to the descriptions, but don't see the art."

"You are not missing much," she confided. The moisture of her breath fell on my ear. She had leaned in to whisper to me, but not touch this time.

"Before," I said, "when you touched me. I felt something."

She giggled again. "Did you?"

I had to laugh, too. How absurd I must sound.

"I have been here long enough," Sola said. "Seen all I need to see." Her voice held a distance in that moment; I don't know if she was talking to me or to herself. "Would you care to escort me out of here, Mr. Werlock?"

"Rafael," I said. "Or Raf, if you please. And yes, I think I'd like to get out of here as well."

On the street, Sola slipped her arm around mine and led me two blocks to a sushi restaurant where we ordered crab eggrolls, crispy calamari, and a tako and ika dish. Delicious. Every morsel. But not as engaging as the evening we shared. A few drinks in—Green Pixies for the lady and Green Dragons for me—I convinced Ms. Sola Pyne to tell me about herself.

"I'm not a very interesting person," she said. "My family is from a small town in Pennsylvania. I moved to Chicago for grad school a couple years ago and met Miranda. We had a class together. Now I work the day shift at the hospital."

"What did you major in?"

"Nursing," she said. "With a minor in art appreciation."

"That explains why you subject yourself to artists."

"My first two years of college I studied psychology—you know, because everybody wants to be a psych major at first, to figure out their own issues, and then to tell everybody else how to fix their lives."

"I was never a psych major," I told her.

"Maybe it's just women then," she said. "But some of that psych stuff still lingers in the back of my mind. I think we never really forget anything we've learned, or experienced. Does that make sense?"

It did. At least, I thought it did. Once you learn something, it's nearly impossible to unlearn it. I thought then of my childhood, the hours spent with my mother as she taught me stories from the Bible, stories I no longer believed in but couldn't forget. I thought of my brother teaching me to shoot a slingshot when I was four and me killing two squirrels; I'd rather not remember that. I could have recited any number of those old stories right then, or loaded a stone into a slingshot and loosed it, though I haven't touched a slingshot in nearly thirty years. Sola was right, as she seemed to always be right: some things stay with us forever. And sometimes that's unfortunate.

"What I am getting at is this," she slurred just a bit. Apparently she was not much of a drinker; somehow, that fact made me more comfortable with her. "I often wonder if the artist is exhibiting the work, or if it's the other way around."

"You think the art reveals the artists?"

"Sure," she said. "What else is art for? It's creation. Isn't the world made in such a way as to reveal the Creator to us? We don't use the Creator to understand the universe; we use the creation to comprehend the Creator."

That was it. The clincher. I didn't believe in Creation. I was of the opinion that we evolved from a pile of cosmic primordial garbage into hyper-complex creatures by a series of random chances and natural stumbling. The idea of a creator was, at that point in my life, ludicrous. But the depth of Sola's logic and the conviction with which she spoke made me a believer in one thing. The one thing I have never questioned.

My love for Sola.

I'm not saying I loved her "at first sight". That would be absurd on multiple levels. But I knew then that I would love her one day soon, and that once I did, I would never be able to stop.

<u>3</u>

A month later we were living together at her place. She had a stable job with steady pay. Her apartment, compared to my little hole-in-the-wall studio, was luxurious. It was roomy and smelled of sandalwood. Incense, Sola told me. Though I couldn't see, I could feel the difference. My old place had been on the north side of a brick building above a bar. Cold and loud. Sola's apartment, henceforth referred to as ours, had plaster walls and sat on the south side of the building. We caught the warmth of the sun morning to night.

On that first night, after we left the restaurant, I'd touched her face. I touched her again on this first night in our new home. That same cold, electrical charge zapped up my arm, but was less intense than it had been when she'd touched me at Mitch Lovecraft's showing. Her face was soft and smooth; her jaw round and small; her lips full and firm. She had a small, pointed nose and small, pointed ears. Like an elf in a fantasy novel. Everything I touched told me that this girl was beautiful. In this regard, my blindness was a blessing. Though I can only feel the beauty of her features, I am as enamored with the physical appeal of women as most men are. Lust is lust. But what you can't see can't stimulate visually. The need in me to see Sola brought forth the need to touch her at every opportunity. Of course, the down side to this is that a blind person must touch to see; and touching, unfortunately, is the catalyst of lust.

I fell in love with Sola, not with her appearance.

So I was shocked when my friends and family began advising me to break off my relationship with her. There were various reasons, but the strangest were these: my brother, Mike, told me that Sola had a "weird" look to her; and my mother bluntly said Sola was a bad girl for me.

"Something is just not right," Mike had said. "She's beautiful. Too beautiful. Like she's not real. There's this weird aura around her. Like a corona. It's…unnatural."

My mother had an opposing view.

"She's an ugly girl. You can do better."

Even Miranda, who had introduced me to Sola that night at Lovecraft's showing, was dead set against our relationship. She opposed my love for Sola so vehemently that she became angry and stormed out of my apartment the day before I had moved, calling me a fool. Nearly six months passed before I heard from her again.

But by that time, I knew more of the truth than any of them could have guessed.

<u>4</u>

It was when I began unpacking my clothes that I found the chest.

I moved in with Sola on a Saturday. She helped me carry the last of my things in, but I was in no rush to unpack. Sola was scheduled long shifts at the hospital, so I'd have all week to get my things in order and familiarize myself with my new home. I'd arranged things so I would not have any deadlines or obligations that first week. Miranda was angry with me for my decision to move in with Sola, so I wouldn't have to worry about any showings in the near future.

Monday came. Sola left for work and I began unpacking my things. After just two nights in the apartment with her, I was feeling at home; like I'd always belonged here with her. Everything felt so right. I still felt that cold shock each time Sola touched me, but my body seemed to be adapting to it. I was thrilled at each embrace, each kiss, each subtle stroke of her hand on my skin; but the jolt was not what it had once been.

Unpacking was not much of a chore. I do not, as a rule, own many things. Mostly I have art supplies— clay, shaping knives, cutting blocks, trimming blades, trimming hooks, sculpting knives, hole cutters, bevel cutters, pin tools, cutting wires—and the few things I use in my writing trade: my laptop , a few notebooks, and a small personal library of braille books. Everything else was toiletries and clothing.

The clothes led me to the chest.

Sola had spent part of Sunday afternoon clearing a closet for me. My closet was the one furthest from the window, closest to the bedroom door.

I laid my suitcase and moving bags on the bed and removed the items in no particular order. With an arm-load of shirts I turned, heading for the closet. As I moved around from my side of the bed, I came to the foot of the bed and banged my shin and knee into something solid. I went down, sprawling on the floor, my shirts falling in a heap beside me. I rolled onto my back and sat up, holding my knee to my chest. Beneath my pants, I could feel the rush of heat as a bruise was conceived. A warm trickle slid down my skin. I had cut my leg on the edge of whatever I'd bumped into.

What the hell did she park there?

But it wasn't her fault. I'd been living as a blind man for many years, so I feel my way everywhere I go. So why not this time? Why had I strolled so haphazardly through this room I had been in only a few times before? Because I was comfortable here, that's why. For the first time since I'd lost my sight, I was content and tranquil. Being in Sola's home, in her life, in her presence, had brought me assurance and hope and peace that I had not felt since my earliest childhood.

So, why did I slam my leg into a stationary object? Simple. Because I'd been walking by memory. That chest had not been there the night before.

Sola had been storing it in the closet that was now mine.

After I'd sat feeling sorry for myself long enough (much longer than necessary), I climbed to one knee and pushed myself to my feet.

Beside me, something hummed.

It reminded me of the sound of a refrigerator turning on, but much louder. Like the buzzing of a million bees. I followed the sound but I didn't have to go far to find it. The noise came from the thing I'd banged into. I assumed it was a table, but the trace of my fingers revealed it to be an enclosed box. Curious, I knelt there before it, feeling my way along its edges and surfaces. The box was cool to the touch and shaped like an old pirate's chest, but made of metal and smelling faintly of alcohol, burning hair and the ocean.

What the hell?

I was drawn to it: compelled to search. It pulled me like gravity; I knew this was something important.

Feeling for the latch, I knelt on my uninjured knee before the chest, and opened the lid.

I'm not one to pry. People have secrets; even in relationships. If Sola had wanted me to know what was in that chest, she would have told me, right? Maybe. Or perhaps she would have left it where I would inevitably trip over it, be overcome with curiosity, and feel the need to pry into her personal stuff.

Well, whatever Sola intended, that's what I did. The lid was open.

A blast of warm, salty air rushed at me. I smelled the ocean, all right; no doubt about it. The odor of burning hair was only on the outside of the box, as was the alcohol smell. The humidity in the room spiked and I began to sweat. My clothes stuck to me. Something in the distance, but from within that mysterious box, called to me. Its language alien. The voice was guttural; thunderous; deeper than Lake Michigan. The voice grew louder as if the thing moved closer to me. That initial blast of sea air now reversed and I was being pulled, sucked into the chest. Had I been on my feet, surely I would have stumbled into that other place—that nexus—and been at the whim of the thing within. But being down on one knee before the open lid stabilized me. I dropped my other knee to the carpet. The blood from the cut had begun to crust to my pant leg and when my knee hit the floor the wound tore open again. I braced myself against the vacuum and slammed the lid shut.

The buzzing stopped. Everything was still except me. I trembled like celestial dew. My chest burned with each breath. The humidity in the room had become as thick as moist clay; I felt like I was breathing in thick gobs of acid.

I got to my feet, stumbled to a window and, pulling it open, thrust my head out into the cold wind of Chicago breathing in the air of my world. I wanted to stay there forever.

The phone rang.

I ignored the first few rings. The machine picked up. "Hello, you have reached Sola…"

Sola…Sola.

Pulled back to reality, I snatched up the phone.

"Hello," I said into the receiver. My voice was ragged. The air had done me good, but my breath was still coming in short gasps.

"Rafael?" Sola said. "What's wrong?"

Quick calculations fired off deep in the back of my mind. Tell her the truth and she will know that I know something very wrong was going on here. She will know I snooped. Sola will leave me. The fear was real. Though she was involved in some bizarre shit— whatever that may be—she was still the best part of my life. I would not risk losing her. I would lie. I'd say that everything was fine; nothing's wrong.

Funny how our mouths and minds seem to never work in harmony.

"What the hell is going on?" I blurted.

"I just called to say hi." Sola sounded hurt.

"There's a chest at the foot of the bed…"

She cut me off.

"You didn't open it, did you?" She did not sound hurt any longer. She was afraid. Panicked.

"I didn't want to," I stuttered. "But I tripped over it and…" I'd said most of that to myself. I don't know how long I'd been talking to the air.

<u>5</u>

Sola burst through the door a half hour later.

"What did you see?" she shouted.

"Nothing," I said.

Neither of us was trying to be funny.

I shook. Probably had for some time.

"There is something in that chest," I said.

She ran to the bedroom. I heard the whirring sound from the chest. The buzzing was louder now. Sola spoke; nearly shouting. Her words in a language foreign to me. A chill crawled along my spine and I had the distinct impression that these words would be alien to anyone on the planet.

I heard Sola return to the living room. Her small, cool hands were on mine. Her soft lips touched my forehead. Then her body was close to mine as she sat next to me on the sofa.

"Do you love me?" she asked.

I hesitated.

"Yes," I said. "I love you."

"There are things about me that few have known. Things I've concealed for a long time."

"We all have secrets," I told her. I had a feeling, though, that Sola's secrets were a shade darker than most people carried.

"If I told you I was different," she said, "Would you still love me?"

"I loved you in the first place because you're different. I love that you are different."

I wondered just what it was we were talking about.

"Are you on the run?" I asked. "You escape from a lab or something?"

"Do you believe there are worlds other than this?" she said.

My turn to sit silently.

Sola answered her question.

"There are, Rafael. There are many worlds that you know nothing of."

"And you're from one of these other worlds?" I asked, incredulous.

Finally I meet the girl of my dreams and she's a total nut. A flake. From another world? Not likely. Living in another world inside her head? Maybe. Damn. I loved that girl. But at this moment, sitting on the couch in her apartment—our apartment now—all I thought was I'd gotten myself involved with a seriously unbalanced woman.

"What's in the box?" I asked.

I listened while Sola took in long breaths. The sound of her chest expanding was eerie, like I was inside a balloon as it was being inflated.

"His name is hard to transliterate into English. The closest sound would be Bloirngik."

I nearly laughed.

She paused again, unsure how to proceed. Maybe she wanted me to say something.

If the experience of the salt-scented chest and the guttural sound in the windy distance had not been so recent, I'm sure I would have scoffed.

"Can we call him Bob?" I asked.

Sola recoiled from me as if I were hideous. Outside the window a bird called to another. Below us in the street, cars sped through the city on the rain-soaked roads. And I was alone again on the couch.

Sola paced.

"You should not mock that which you do not understand," she said. Her voice was harsh, wounded. "I was sure your mind was more expanded than most humans."

At that word—*humans*—my skin tingled.

"What do you mean?" I muttered. Like a scolded child, I spoke softly, apologetically.

"You are an artist, Rafael. You have had an open mind since the day we met, but now you scoff and mock me when the truth is laid bare before you."

"I'm sorry," I said.

"There is great revelation all around you, Rafael. You need only try to see it and you will."

I pointed to my vacant eyes.

"I don't know about that," I said.

"Your sight is a trivial problem." She spoke softly now. Her smooth hand was on mine. The weight of her body comforting next to mine. "You do not need sight to have vision."

"That's deep," I said. "But still, sight wouldn't hurt. You wouldn't happen to have anything back on your home world that can cure blindness, would you?"

She did not answer but leaned close to me and, pressing her head to my chest, wrapped her slender arms around me.

"Tell me about this Biorn—" I tried, but I could not pronounce the strange word.

"Bloirngik."

"Right. Will you tell me about him? Or her?"

"Will you believe me?"

"I'll believe whatever you tell me."

"Even if it's unbelievable?"

"I may require some proof," I said.

"You won't like it," she said.

"The truth?"

"The proof."

6

"What is it?"

We were in the bedroom. Together. It occurred to me that this was the first time we'd been together in the bedroom since my first night in this apartment. I stood before the chest, listening to the continuous hum, Sola standing at my side.

"A containment device," she said.

"Like on Ghostbusters?"

"I am not familiar with Ghostbusters," she said.

"Okay," I said, "that's all the proof I need. You're from another world, all right."

I remember that look my mother used to give me when I said something she couldn't find a response to. I imagine Sola glaring at me with the same mixture of love and consternation right then. That look on mom's face is one of the last things I remember seeing before I lost my sight. That, and Ghostbusters.

"What does it contain?" I asked.

"An artificial realm made to hold one being."

"A prison?"

"Not quite. A life-support station."

It's hard to pinpoint a moment when I truly started to believe Sola was not human, not of this world, but if any one moment could be named, it would be this one. She spoke with such nonchalance, such certainty, like someone giving directions to a place they've been to a million times.

"And it's supporting Bilon—"

"Bloirngik," she said. "Yes. He needs a very specific living environment."

"But why are you here with him? Who are you to him? How are the two of you related?"

"It is complicated."

"Un-complicate it for me," I suggested.

"You could call me his nurse," she said.

"You care for him?"

"Yes?"

"Why?"

"I healed his illness. Now he is dying. I provide him with as much comfort as I can. It is what I was made to do."

"You're a hospice nurse," I said. It wasn't so much a question, as a revelation spoken aloud. Here on Earth—in this life she'd made—Sola worked as a nurse, spending much of her time comforting the dying. It had never occurred to me that she did this on a galactic scale.

I took her silence to mean she did not understand.

"Hospice is a special kind of care given to those who are dying. To make them comfortable at the end of their lives. Like you're doing."

"I did not know humans had such a thing," she said.

"What was his illness?"

"He had a type of radiation poisoning."

"And you can heal that?"

"It is what I was designed to do."

"Can all of your race do this?"

All of her race? What the hell was I talking about?

"I am all of my race," she said.

"You're the last of your kind?"

"I am the first of my kind."

"Where did you come from?"

"A world unlike this one. Far away. Beyond the stars. Beyond the mind."

"Another planet?"

From within the chest I heard the waves of an enormous ocean crashing into a distant shore. And beyond that, a deep, rumbling sigh followed by a noise like a landslide and a splash like tsunami.

Sola gripped my arm and warmth flowed through me. I became drowsy, as if drugged.

"Go lie on the sofa," she told me.

I went to the sofa and laid down.

When I woke, Sola was in the room with me. She sat in the chair near the end of the couch, breathing heavily. Sobbing softly.

"What is it?" I said.

"He's gone."

"I'm sorry."

"I do what I can," Sola said," but in the end, they always die."

"Everyone dies," I said. "No one can escape death." I sat up, shook the sleep from my head, wiped the sleep from my eyes.

"That doesn't make it easier," she said.

"No. Death is never easy. Not for those left living."

We sat in silence for a long time. I felt the heat of the sun through the window behind me. At that angle, I guessed the time to be about four o'clock. I'd slept a couple hours. My mind was slow with sleep but the memories of my morning were coming back and with them, the questions.

"What did you do to me?"

"Nothing." There was dismay in her voice, as if I'd offended her with my allegation. "What do you mean?"

"You told me to lie down on the couch, you said it like a command, and I obeyed like I was hypnotized."

"Not a command," she said softly. "Not hypnosis either. A suggestion. A power given to me by the Designer to bring calm into stressful situations."

"You manipulated me."

"No. Just your mind."

"My mind is me," I said, nearly yelling.

"No." She laughed lightly. "No, my dear Rafael. You are so much more. Humans have such a limited view of themselves. I have listened for many years to people describing themselves. They title themselves with narrow terms and labels that fit the moment. When a woman gives birth she calls herself a mother and forever after that is how she thinks of herself. Is she more than that or only that? Is she not also a dancer, a singer, a walker, or a consumer, or a speaker, a praiser, or learner, or any number of unlimited things? And why is a man defined by his work only? Ask a man who he is and what will he say? Who are you, Rafael?"

"I'm me," I said.

"But what does that mean?"

"It means I am. I simply am. My name is Rafael Werlock."

"Indeed it is. But is that who you are? Are you not more than a name?"

"I'm a sculptor," I said.

"That is but one thing you do. What if you could

not sculpt, or chose not to? Would you still be?"

"Of course."

"Then you are more than one aspect of yourself?"

"Yes," I said. "Of course I am."

"Then you are more than your mind, though your mind is part of you."

"Still," I said, growing irritated, "you manipulated me. You violated my trust."

"I am sorry you feel that way," she said. "I am sorry if I have hurt you or harmed our relationship."

Our relationship was another issue altogether. I'd had a hell of a morning by this point. An alien being trapped in a chest in the bedroom had died and I was being told that the love of my life was an alien too.

This is the kind of shit that makes people crazy.

"Promise me you'll never do that to me again."

"All right," she said. "I will never calm you again."

Calm? Manipulate? Violate an unspoken trust agreement? I wasn't going to argue semantics.

"Before you *calmed* me," I said, "you were telling me that you're from another world?"

"That's right."

I heard the rustling of her clothes, felt the shift in the air as she stood. Her footfalls were soft as she tread the carpet. She paced. I remained seated, though I was restless.

"You're from another planet?"

"In a manner of speaking."

"It seems to me that it's a pretty cut and dry question, Sola. Are you from earth or not?"

"I did not originate on Terra."

I didn't say anything. Through the thick air in the

78

room, I sensed Sola struggle to say the right thing. I waited, impatient and curious, full of wonder, like a young man witnessing birth. I found myself believing every word she was saying, and all the things she was implying.

"I come from a world that is my world," she said.

"You mean a world that was made for you? Or a world that you made? Or a world you just happen to have been born on? I don't follow."

"All of these things are accurate."

"Either it was made for you by someone else," I said," or you made it. Can't be both."

"But it can," she said. "All beings exist in worlds within others and yet they create their own worlds within.

"Think of all the races of humans on Terra. Think of Terra itself. Is Terra a world? Yes. But on the surface of Terra are there not many worlds? Think of the street people in the slums of Chicago and compare them to the street people of India. Think of a pub owner in Ireland or a fisherman in China. Monks in Tibet or priests in the Vatican. Cab drivers and policemen. Prostitutes and nuns. These are more than variations in lifestyles and choices and cultures: these are worlds within worlds.

"The same variations of worlds exist in this universe and beyond."

"You're talking about different dimensions?"

"I am trying to help you understand that there is more to reality than what you perceive. There are worlds piled upon worlds and worlds beyond those. You have your own world, Rafael. We each have our own world. Our worlds overlap sometimes and we fall into someone else's world. Is this one yours or mine? I do not know. Maybe neither. Maybe we have each fallen from our worlds into the world of someone we both know, or someone neither of us knows. The Designer has created many worlds and many beings. For the most part, certain beings belong to certain places, certain realms or planes or planets or dimensions. Call them what you will. The fact is this, there are worlds other than this one. I am from one of them."

"How did you come to this world?" I asked her.

"Bloirngik called out to the Designer. He was in pain and dying and needed help. I heard him and was transported to him."

"He was on earth?"

"No. He was in a vessel heading for this world."

"The chest?" I was amazed. Could this be true? Was this metal box in the bedroom an interstellar spaceship designed by an alien race?

"Yes," she said.

"How did you board his ship? Do you have a vessel of your own?"

"I have no ship. So great was Bloirngik's pain that he called me across time and space to himself."

"You can be summoned?" I asked. "Like a genie from a lamp?"

"Not quite." Sola chuckled. The sound of her laughter lightened my mood. "When pain is great enough I am drawn to it, the way a shark is drawn to blood."

"So you took away his pain?"

"I healed his illness."

"Can you cure anything? I mean, does it have to be disease or sickness? Can you repair damage to a body?"

The thought leaped into my mind unbidden.

Suddenly I was on my feet, pacing. I couldn't keep still. It was like I was six years old again and waiting for mom to get home so I could tell her what I really wanted—more than anything in the world—for Christmas.

In my frantic realization, my excitement, I'd forgotten Sola was on her feet as well. I slammed into her, nearly knocking her off her feet. I caught her by her arms, held her upright. Her body tensed, her arms tightened beneath my grip.

"Can you make me see?" The words pounced from my mouth. "Can you cure my blindness?"

I relaxed my grip.

"I'm sorry," I said. "Did I hurt you?"

"Sola, all my life I've wanted my sight back. I've begged and pleaded and prayed and never did I get any kind of answer. Then you drop into my life with these wild tales and I'm desperate enough to believe you. If you can make me see, do it. Please do it. I'd give anything to see again."

When she spoke, her voice was distant and sad; like a whisper cast into the wind. "You do not know what you are asking."

"Can you heal me?"

"Yes," she said. She brushed my hands. "But I love you."

"If you love me, do this for me." I was begging. All pride and dignity had fled. After all these long years, my prayers were answered.

"There is a price for all things," she said.

"I'll pay it." Beyond my pleading was a greed, an eagerness that I'd never heard in my voice. Inside, there was such hope, such desire as I'd never felt before.

"Do not stop loving me," she said.

"Never," I said.

And then she kissed me.

Her lips were wet. Not moist: wet. As if she were excreting some kind of venom from her mouth and passing it into mine with her passion. This kiss was the most wonderful thing I'd felt in all my life. I'd never experienced anything so erotic. The taste was exotic. Like bitter fruit roasted over star fire.

There was an abrupt explosion in my mouth: like a thousand suns bursting into existence on my tongue. Each one moved. It felt like an egg sac had ruptured and a million spider hatchlings scampered through my insides. I was terrified.

Repulsed, I wanted to reel away but Sola's kiss, her touch, held me in place.

Inside, the crawling things ran down my throat and clambered up into my nasal cavity. I was overcome with the need to sneeze and to vomit, but could do neither as I felt them dive into my bloodstream and burrow into every inch of me. They were searching for something, I thought. Digging through my body like treasure hunters. The sensation was that of stinging gnats swarming, but all on the inside. I wanted to fall to the ground, roll around, and crush each one of them, jump about and dance the way you do when a bee flies into your shirt.

But still I could not move. I stood rigid, caught in Sola's spell.

They reached my brain. Pain erupted in my skull as if these creatures blasted their way through with dynamite.

Sola did not stop kissing me. She held my face in her hands, gently, continuing to press her warm lips to mine.

The smell of singed flesh filled my nostrils. Or maybe the scent was only in my mind. The taste of copper and salt settled on my tongue. A heavy film clung like plastic to the roof of my mouth. Into my ears came a rush of wind carrying a tune played on an instrument made of steel from a world a thousand light years away.

I was at peace in my pain.

Sola pulled her lips from mine.

"I will miss you," she whispered.

There came a final burst of cosmic pain in the galaxy of my head. My eyes shot open.

7

Blue.

The walls of Sola's apartment were blue. Soft blue, like the sky on a clear day. The carpet was a stark white, like a field a snow. It ended at the kitchen floor: smooth wood in shades of brown and lines of black.

I went through the cupboards. The peanut butter was brown but not like the wood of the floors, and the lid of the jar a bright red. The label had bright yellow lettering and I couldn't take my eyes off it for a long time. I lingered in the kitchen, trying to read the labels of the various containers, but couldn't make sense of the shapes of the letters that I hadn't seen in more than two decades. The items in the refrigerator I tasted so often were foreign to me. I had nearly forgotten the way an apple's skin shines in the light.

The light from the window brought me back to the living room. I gazed out the window, opened it, and stuck my head out. The building across the way was one of those old brick buildings, red and enormous. I stared at a single brick. The red was faded in spots. There were gray specks in the little indentations shining like tiny diamonds in the glaring sun. The mortar between the bricks was a putrid grey running in lines as far as I could see.

I could see!

At the window I stood for a long time, gazing down at the people going by. The yellow taxis buzzed among the traffic. Street vendors stood at intervals along the sidewalks, calling out to pedestrians among the bustle of the afternoon, there stalls and carts adorned with brightly colored parasols of red and blue and white and yellow. So much color. So much sight to take in. Beyond the multitude of people and vehicle, I could see the lake shore and highway. The fields beyond the city lay beyond the bustle of Chicago but I saw them as if I they were only a block down. Not only could I see, I could see more clearly, more vividly, than I recall seeing in my childhood. Everything was so real. Whatever Sola had done had not only repaired my sight, it made it keener than a human's sight is meant to be.

I reveled in the wonder of the world.

My world.

I turned to Sola.

She sat in her chair. The big comfortable thing with fluffy cushions and wide arms. It was blue cloth. Expensive. Sola sat with her feet pulled up under her like a child. I looked at her then, for the first time. Enthralled with my new sight, I not taken a moment to just look at her. Now I did.

She was beautiful. Her skin a milky brown like caramel poured over whipped cream. I had felt her long hair a hundred times, running my fingers through it as she lay next to me, petting it softly. But now I looked on it: the ebon locks hanging passed her shoulder, shining in the sunlight streaming in through the open windows. Her features appeared as small and delicate as I they had felt on my fingertips. High cheekbones and soft skin; a small round nose and wide red mouth; a little pointed chin; and big eyes that shone such a soft grey I would never have imagined had I not seen them.

Those round grey eyes watched me. She was sad. I could tell. She was gorgeous, even in her sadness.

"What's wrong?"

"I do not want to lose you," she said.

"Are you kidding? You'll never lose me, baby. A week ago I would have said you've made me the happiest man in the world." I went to her, knelt before her, took her hand in mine and looked up into her face, smiling. She did not smile. "Now what can I say? Not only are you perfect, you've opened my eyes. You've done what no one else could ever do."

"You do not know what I have done," she said. "But I want you to know I am sorry."

"Sorry? For what? Don't be sorry, Sola. I'm so happy right now I could explode. You've changed my life."

"I should not have done that. It was weakness."

"I don't know what you mean."

She gazed down at me, kneeling there before her like I was proposing. Her grey eyes shifted in the light. Flashed. Green then blue. An angry red raced through them and was gone. Then there were the grey pools again, but darker than before.

"When we experience things with another," she said, "we only experience half of them. When I heal, I only feel it from my side. I have no concept of how the healing feels to the infected."

"It feels—"

She pressed a slender finger to my lips. "I do not know how it feels. But I know what it leads to."

Sola paused. I think she was waiting for my mind to catch up, waiting for me to piece things together. Maybe I was getting there. Inside, I probably always knew. From the moment Bloirngik died I think I always knew.

"You will die," she said.

She didn't break down the way women do. Not Sola. Her eyes each loosed a single stream of tears that ran to her narrow chin and dripped onto her lap, onto our joined hands.

My mouth was dry.

We all die. I know that. I've always known.

"How long?" I asked.

"I don't know." Her voice did not shake.

"Will I know when it's coming?"

"There be will pain," she said. "There is always pain. Like a cancer spreading through you."

"How does your power to heal bring about cancer?" I asked.

"It is a safety mechanism created by the Designer. The bacteria my body produces can repair damage and cure illness. All kinds known across the universes. But all things must die. That is the way of all life."

"So if you heal someone, you heal all their ailments?"

"The bacteria repair all damage. They restore all cells to their optimum state. But those bacteria—what you call my power—do not die until the host creature dies. They gather and stagnate, causing a blockage in an organ that will shut down the host's body, eventually."

"They're parasites?"

"Of a kind. Yes."

"I kind of wish we'd had this chat before that kiss," I said.

"I am sorry." She turned away from me.

I stood. Went to the window. The cool breeze brushed my skin. The sun descended at the far end of the city. Long shadows stretched out past the horizon. I looked beyond them and saw a glimpse of my future. Life would go on with renewed vigor. My work would evolve. My art was meant to encompass all things, not just sculpting. Now I could paint and draw and do anything my heart led me to do. And Sola would be there with me. We'd be happy, together. Sola and I would have each other. Until the end.

I went to her.

"Thank you." I looked down at her.

Her face was turned away. She did not look at me.

"I mean it. Thank you. I have what I've always wanted." I put my hand under her wet chin, turned her face gently to me.

"It was impulsive," she said.

"Because you love me."

"I was reckless with you."

"I'm glad you were."

She turned her face toward me. Where the tears streaked down her soft cheeks, hard cracks bore into her brown skin. From within those cracks shone a radiant blue. Like phosphorescent fish glowing beneath the surface of calm water, Sola's true self became visible to me only through her sadness.

"What is it?" she said. Her eyes were wide. She

looked up at me as I stumbled backward. "Why are you looking at me that way?"

"Your tears," I said.

She touched her face. Moist brown skin rubbed off onto her fingertips. It was thick, like frosting on a cake. She looked at the clump of material on her hand. It was melting, dripping onto the floor. Sola's big eyes, bloodshot with those luminous blue streaks, stared up at me beseechingly. She looked like a child caught in the act, expecting punishment.

Where she touched her face, the thick, gelatinous make-up wiped away. Beneath her eyes, high on her cheeks, I saw the soft glow of her true flesh. Sola's true beauty. Her true self that she had hidden all her days on earth.

<u>8</u>

Explaining my miraculous healing was easy. Making people believe me was not.

My story was simply. Remember that episode of Little House when Mary woke up blind? Just for no reason, she woke up one morning and could not see. Nobody could explain it. Act of God, right? Sure. Well, my situation was like that. I woke up one morning and—bam!—I could see. Believe me, I'm more amazed than anyone.

Most people seemed to buy it, at least on the surface.

Some were skeptical.

A medical experiment? Was it some new procedure, perhaps? A secret government thing? Nope. Just happened. Act of God. And I'm very grateful, believe me. I've been wishing and hoping and praying for this my whole life.

"What?" Miranda had asked me. "You prayed?"

We were speaking again. She missed me, she wanted me to know. It's just that this relationship with Sola was such a whirlwind affair, the way the two of us had been utterly consumed with one another, ignoring and neglecting our responsibilities to those around us. I had missed two lunch dates with Miranda and one with Kevin Guft during the first two weeks of dating Sola. This was the reason that Miranda had tried to warn me away from Sola. Sola was bad for my career; bad for my social life. As I was bad for hers. Miranda was adamant about this. Also, we had offended Mitch Lovecraft—Sola and I—when we had left his showing early. Our absence had been noted.

"Sure," I said. "I pray, sometimes. Everybody does. I don't care what they say. When a man wants something bad enough and that thing, whatever it may be, remains consistently out of reach, he'll pray."

"But you're an atheist," Miranda said.

"Am I?"

We were sitting in a booth at a corner bar downtown. Miranda had invited me to lunch and drinks. Always drinks. Miranda wore a yellow sundress bright as the sun. Her hair was brown and frazzled. I had known this woman for years and had never looked on her face. She had a round face with smooth skin. Very feminine. Pretty. Her skin was that color of pink-white you get when you haven't been outside in a month.

"Ever since I've known you," Miranda said, "you've never believed in God."

"Well," I said. "What can I say? I once was lost, but now I'm found." I smiled.

"Funny," she said. "Look, Raf. Mitch Lovecraft is having another showing in two weeks."

I scoffed. The beer was warm and flat but I drank it anyway. My eyes lingered on the amber liquid and the white foam, avoiding Miranda's gaze.

"Come on," she said, leaning forward. "He likes you. And he respects you. You really hurt him last time when you walked out like that."

"It's been nearly six months," I said. "I'm sure he's over it."

"I'm sure he is not." Miranda lit a cigarette. I watched the tip ignite in an orange glow and followed the white smoke with my eyes as it drifted up past the NO SMOKING sign. "But look, Raf. Do it for me, will you? Hell, do it for yourself. You're still part of the community. You've just been on hiatus for a while."

"Speaking of which," she said, "we should be putting together a showing for you pretty soon."

"I've got a couple pieces done," I told her. "A sculpture from clay and a marble piece that's nearly finished. A few paintings—"

"You're painting?"

I pointed to my eyes and said, "I thought I'd give it shot. I'll bring one by sometime for you."

Miranda looked at her cellphone.

"I've got to get going," she said. "Give Sola my love."

Miranda slid out of the booth. I followed, leaving a wad of cash on the table.

"Let me walk you out," I said.

Outside, I hailed a cab for Miranda.

"You want to share?" she asked, sliding to the far side.

"No, thanks. I'll walk. See the sights."

She smiled.

"I'm so happy for you," she said.

"Thanks."

"Don't forget the showing. I'll send you a message with the details."

The cab pulled away. Miranda shoved her head out the window and shouted to me. "Bring Sola to the showing."

"Will do," I said to the wind.

2

The first headache came in the middle of the night.

Ten days after my sight returned, I woke in the dark, screaming. Pain inside my head brought me fully awake. I was sitting up, my head in my hands. It felt like something was worming through my brain, eating its way through me.

Sola was there. Sola was always there. She held me. Her thin arms kept me steady as I shook. There in the dark, she laid me out, pressing me roughly to the mattress, pinning me down with a supernatural strength.

"It will pass," she whispered.

And it did.

I woke before dawn. She was not beside me. I found her in the living room. She stood naked before the big window. The sun not yet risen, the moon not yet gone. Sola's back and legs where straight and rigid and covered in wicked scars. She stood like a sentry keeping watch, her head tilted up as if watching the sky.

"What is it?" I asked.

"The sickness is settling into you."

I had gathered as much. But that was not what I'd meant.

"I mean, what is it you're looking for?"

"I'm listening," she said.

I stepped to the shadows of the darkened room.

A beam of moonlight flowed down upon Sola, bathing her in white light. She was naked in the truest sense. The creamy brown make-up was gone from her body. She had the shape of a woman, the curves of the body I had come to know well, but from head to foot she was fluorescent blue, except for the white streaks of scar tissue on her back and thighs. She shimmered in the light of the moon. So beautiful. Her long dark hair was gone, replaced with a smooth baldness.

"What are these scars?" I asked her.

"Souvenirs from a time I would rather forget. Cruelty I do not wish to speak of."

"What do you hear when you listen?"

"The pain of the universe. I hear calls from the desperate throughout all the worlds."

"Like the call you heard that brought you to Bloirngik?" I asked.

She did not answer.

I put my arms around her waist, closed my hands on hers.

"Some," she said. "Others are like the calls that brought me here, to your world."

"There were calls from Earth?"

"There are always calls from Earth, Rafael," she said. "At all times. Terra is home to an abundance of suffering. Humans cry out constantly. Your calls were among them."

"What calls? When did I call out?"

"In the night, when you are alone, when you are

desperate, do you not call out for the things you want most? Many of the calls are but whispers, but each comes to me the same."

"Do you mean…prayers? You hear people's prayers?"

"I hear those in pain."

"But you can't possibly answer all the prayers of the world."

"No," she whispered. "Not all. And not only what you call prayers, but the yearning of all things in pain."

"How do you choose?"

Sola turned to me, surprise in her soft grey eyes. We stood facing each other in the moonlight.

"Choose? I do not choose, Rafael. When pain is too much and desperation enough, I am summoned. And when I am summoned, I go."

"But you chose me. Right? You came here to heal me."

"I came here because I was called to Bloirngik and his vessel was coming to this planet. When I arrived on this world there were so many voices calling—so much pain on this planet—that I could feel the summoning all around me. Then a voice broke through and summoned me. I went to it and helped it. I met you between summonings. I'm glad I did."

"Are you being summoned now?"

"I am being summoned always."

"Then you will go?"

"Yes."

"Can't you choose to stay?"

"I do not choose. When a summoning occurs, I will be taken."

"Taken? Like an abduction?"

A weak smile creased her lips.

"Something like that," she said.

"Can I come with you?" I asked.

"No. Only this world is suitable for you. You would not survive anywhere else."

"I'll die soon anyway," I said.

"You cannot travel as I do, Rafael."

"Tell me about it. How you travel."

"Humans would call it teleportation, because they have no other word for it. I move at speeds beyond anything your people can understand. It takes eight minutes for light to travel from your sun to your world. If I am summoned now, I will be there now."

"How is that possible?"

"I told you once before, there are worlds other than this one. Many beings exist in those worlds. I am unique in that I do not exist in any world, yet I exist in all. I can be in all places instantly, but not all places at once."

"Then you are God?" I was astounded, standing in a room with—

"No." She laughed. "I am not God. I am not a god. I am what I am. No more, no less. I was created by the Designer, just like all other things."

"But you are omnipresent?"

"I can be called to any place at any time, crossing the barriers of time and space and dimension. But I cannot be in all places. And I cannot choose when to travel."

"You're stuck here until you're summoned somewhere else?"

"Yes."

"When will that happen?"

"I cannot tell you. I am always being called.

When a summoning occurs, I will be taken from this place to another. Though I was hoping to stay here quite a while longer."

She kissed me.

We stayed in the moonlight, holding each other, until the moonlight was gone.

10

The headaches got worse.

I was in my studio, working. We'd torn out the carpet in the second bedroom and turned the place into an artist's dream. I was standing at my workbench, chiseling out the last details, what I'd hoped would be the last details, of a small marble statuette, when the boring sensation came inside my skull.

I collapsed.

The marble statuette, meant to be an image of Sola, crashed down on me. I felt a rib break. The air was knocked from me. The statuette tumbled to the hardwood floor and broke into a dozen pieces.

Instantly the pain in my head shifted. I felt the crawling of the spider things—what Sola had named bacteria—scrambling down my throat and into my chest.

Tearing my shirt open, I watched in terror as a mass formed under the flesh of my chest. A huge lump swelled. Burning agony stole through me as the things went to work within me once more.

I heard the bone snap back into place, felt it mending. Where the jagged edges of the rib had torn my insides, the creatures within were quick to repair the damage.

Then it was over. I was fine. I sat up on the hard floor, feeling the scuttling and clambering of the bacteria up through my body and into my throat. Impulse gripped me. Grabbing a long brush, I dipped the bristles into a glob of white paint, breaking through the air-hardened shell into the still moist material within the bubble. I rammed the tip of the brush to the back of my throat. I needed to see. I steeled myself. When I pulled the brush out, I was not prepared.

There were a dozen of them trapped in the sticky white paint. They were blue. And glowing. Tiny organisms with a multitude of limbs. I was repulsed and fascinated. These things disgusted me. Yet, I loved them. They were part of Sola. Her gift to me. So that she would always be part of me. And though I loved her and them by association, I wanted the things out of me.

The thought came to me that if I could get them out, all of them, then they could not linger and fester and kill me. If I could bait the creatures out of my body, I could retain the sight they'd given me without fear of death creeping up on me. Why should I endure these chronic headaches needlessly? Why should I dread the death these things would inevitably carry me to?

I grabbed a clean paintbrush and dipped into the white paint, ready to trap them, to catch them in the gooey paint and drag them from my body. They weren't moving now. They'd scuttled back to wherever they dwell and were motionless. I had to find a way to get them moving again. Using a trimming blade from my sculpting table, I sliced a long gash across the back of my forearm. Warm pain erupted in my arm as blood splatted a half-finished canvas.

Instantly I felt them moving inside me. I plunged the second paintbrush to the back of my throat, this time much harder than I intended, and triggered my gag reflex. A spray of vomit followed the brush out of my mouth. On the tip of the paintbrush I'd caught another mass of them and the puddle of vomit was teeming with blue movement.

As they closed up the cut in my arm I ripped a piece of paper towel from the roll and dabbed the rapidly healing wound. When I pulled the paper towel away, dozens of the insect-like things came off, writhing in the absorbed pool of my blood. Fascinated by this discovery, and by the prospect of saving myself from the death these creatures would bring me, I reached for a cutting wire, intending to slice a wide swath of flesh from my torso.

My fascination was short lived and my plan interrupted, as the tiny creatures finished the climb back to their nest. My head swam with pain. I may have screamed. Probably I did. But I don't remember. Everything went black and I feared that my sight had been taken from me again. As the wound on my arm closed, a last drop of blood fell to the floor and I fell with it.

11

Sola knelt over me. She wore her brown face. The shadows coming through the window were much longer now. How long was I out?

"What have you done?" Sola said, looking down at me. "You must not remove the bacteria from your body."

"Why not?" I asked. "If they're killing me, why not try to remove them so I can live?"

"They are a part of you now, Rafael. They are one with you even as they are one with me. Those that dwell within you cannot live with you; neither can you live without them. They will cause your death eventually, but separating them from you will kill you immediately."

I laid there, staring into her eyes, not saying a word.

"Did you have another headache?" Sola asked me.

"Yes. They're getting worse."

"Yes," she said. "They will get worse. For a while. Then they may cease, or may not. Often they will settle into the host and bond cohesively. If this is the case, the pain will end permanently. This is not always the case. The bacteria bond differently with various species, and individuals. I have seen many humans suffer greatly from the bacteria, while others showed no signs of pain."

"You've spent a lot of time among humans?"

"Yes. I am summoned to Terra often."

I stood and followed Sola into the living room. She went to the window, looked up into the sky again, as if waiting for the sun to vanish and the stars to come out. But that time was still hours away.

"How are you feeling now?" she asked.

"Fine. Feel like I've slept for a week. Fully refreshed."

"I am glad," she said. "What time is Lovecraft's showing?"

"Seven o'clock, I think. But that's not today, is it?"

"Yes," Sola said. "If you are really feeling all right, you should get yourself ready. We should be going soon."

I showered quickly and shaved. The clock on the bathroom wall said six-fifteen. Time to head out. I expected Sola to be sitting on the couch, waiting for me. She was not. I called out to her. No answer. I went to the bedroom. She was not there. Into the kitchen, the second bathroom. She was nowhere. I panicked. She was gone. It had happened. She'd been summoned.

A sound from my studio.

I ran into the room.

There she was. Sola. Thank God. She was on one knee, cleaning up broken pieces of marble.

"I was calling to you," I said.

"I am sorry," she said. "There are so many voices calling to me, I did not realize one of them was you."

She stood and looked at me. Her smile at that moment was the greatest thing I've ever seen. I will never forget it.

"I was afraid you'd gone," I said, panting.

"Not yet, my love."

I went to her, desperate to have her in my arms. But my desperation was weaker than another's. At that moment, as I felt the warmth of her body pressed against mine, the windows in the room shook and the pressure around me shifted. My ears popped. Sola Pyne vanished. Time blinked and Sola was gone.

12

As promised, I showed up to Mitch Lovecraft's showing at seven o'clock. Though I hadn't wanted to go in the first place, I sure didn't want to be there now, without Sola.

Dorian DeWeerd

I walked through the gallery like a zombie, not focusing on anything, mingling as little as possible. Of course Miranda Stotch and Kevin Guft pulled me into a long conversation, introducing me to a number of local artists and aficionados that I had no interest in meeting on my best day. And Mitch Lovecraft wanted to shake my hand and express to me how much he respected my work and he was a big admirer, et cetera. I wasn't listening. He must have picked up on it, because he didn't hang around long.

I explained away Sola's absence with a story of illness. Funny, now that I think about it.

Once I got away from the crowd, I made my way to the far side of the room where large paintings lined a windowless brick wall. On the far left, I found a picture larger than many of the others, entitled "Birth of the Eldest." It depicted a huge creature with a cephalopod face and weird black wings stretching out inside a globe of gold set against a black background. The creature's skin was a putrid green surrounded by a soft green glow.

The piece Miranda had described for me the night I'd met Sola.

I moved to the next picture.

Head throbbing, breath caught in my chest, I stood in awe before this fantastic work of art.

The painting was of an alien spacecraft, cross-sectioned so the viewer could look inside. In the pilot's seat of the cross-sectioned craft sat a large, motionless figure. It was old and made of a gelatinous scale hide, like a soft exoskeleton. From the end of four multi-segmented forelimbs extended large claws manipulating a variety of devices. Its hideous cephalopod face was contorted in agony; its lone protuberant eye was shot through with blue streaks as if bloodshot. The lower portion of the face melded into a pointed beak made of a shiny black substance like jellied oil. The creature had no legs, or what I would call legs, but a massive bundle of dark, slimy tentacles curled beneath it in that crude seat.

The detail of the painting was superb.

Not just the one painting. As I pulled my eyes reluctantly from the first, I realized that it was one in a series lined along the wall. Above the row of paintings stood a long plaque bearing the title of the series: "The Rescue of the Traveler Out of Time."

I looked back to the first painting. Studied it. A small plaque beneath bore a title familiar and disturbing. I stopped, my heart skipped weirdly in my chest. There before me was a name I never thought to see in print. The grotesque piece displayed before me depicted a scene from a story I had heard not so long before.

I was witnessing "The Suffering of Bloirngik."

I slowly moved to the next; my eyes not quite ready to abandon the first. But my mind and my heart, were ready to search for the image I knew I would find somewhere in this series of bizarre pictures.

Third painting from the end. Descending in a flowing white garment like an angel or a bride in the upper left hand corner, a radiant blue figure was emerging from the depths of space.

Second from the end. Fully visible now, the figure was transcending the space outside the ship with the space inside. It was clear this was Sola in her true form, as I had seen her that night, naked in the moonlight. The white garment flowed around her image as she passed through the vessel's wall. The painting was done expertly and in such a way that Sola was standing in both places—inside and outside the ship—at the same time. She was defying the laws of space. The garment, a thin white dress, seemed to be alive and flowing though it was nothing but paint on the canvas.

The last picture was beautiful and grotesque. Here was Sola Pyne, the real Sola Pyne, as few knew her, leaning over the bloated figure of the repugnant squid-faced beast she'd called Bloirngik. He was enormous, even in the picture. Sola's slender frame hovered above him; her lips pressed against his shining black beak; her body was less than a fourth of his mass.

A voice spoke behind me.

"Do you like it?" Mitch Lovecraft found me once again.

I turned on him, frantic and confused.

"How did you see this?" I said. "Where did this come from?"

"What do you mean?" Lovecraft said.

"How did you create such a thing?"

Lovecraft shuffled a step away from me. "You wouldn't believe me." "Tell me," I pleaded.

"Okay," he said. "Just relax. Look, I knew this girl once and she told me this story about a woman she'd met-"

"Did she know the woman's name?"

"She never told me a name. It was just a story the woman had told her. A story about an alien who travels through time and space to help people. People and aliens. Whatever. Just a story, you know?"

"Who was the girl?"

Lovecraft stood dumb, his mouth opened and closed but released no sound.

"The girl who told you the story," I said. "Who was she?"

He remained silent, but his eyes betrayed him. Lovecraft was glancing to his left. I followed his eyes. Across the room, Miranda had stopped conversing and was watching my exchange with Lovecraft with more than passing interest.

"No," I gasped. "Miranda?"

"Listen, Mr. Werlock." The smug bastard was always so damned respectful. "We were out for drinks one night and when we walked outside she pointed at the stars and said that she knew a woman from out there. Just drunk talk, right?"

"Why didn't she tell me?"

"Tell you?" Lovecraft sputtered. "Tell you what? Look, man, I don't know what this is all about, but you're freaking me out."

He backed away, looked at me like I was a madman.

I muttered an apology and took a step back.

Miranda was hurrying toward me. Her heels clicking and echoing like they had on the night I'd met Sola.

I left Mitch Lovecraft there, standing before the display of Sola Pyne.

Only Miranda tried to stop me as I fled the room, fled the building, and ran into the street. Dusk had come and gone, darkness had settled in for the night. The streets were bustling with people living their lives, going about their business and pleasures, some content, some not. I stopped on the wide sidewalk and let the traffic of human beings flow around me like an ageless rock in a river of humanity. In the dark sky I saw the infinite smattering of stars beyond the lights of the city. Distant stars with planets and moons circling them. Was it one of those planets that Sola went? How could I know?

I knew at that moment I'd never see her again; never hold her again and listen to her heavenly breathing while she slept. The sight she'd restored to me was no blessing without her. I'd give it away—go back to my life of blindness—if it meant I could have her back. Would infecting myself with an affliction bring her back to me? But what sickness could I inflict upon myself that would cause me to cry loud enough to call Sola Pyne back into my life?

Nothing. Damn it. There is no illness that can ever afflict me now that Sola's healing power lay within me. Sola's bacteria will keep me healthy until they kill me.

Maybe Miranda would have the answer. It was not easy for me to accept that she had known the truth of Sola's nature from the beginning. Somehow she had drawn Sola to herself and then led us to one another. Hadn't she? Maybe not. Just then, things were beginning to make sense to me. I was beginning to understand why Miranda had been so opposed to my relationship with Sola. Miranda was my friend. She had been protecting me from the inevitable pain that would come once Sola was summoned and taken from me. I resolved to ask Miranda to tell me the truth, everything she knew about Sola; but I would have to wait until the pain of Sola's absence waned.

I stood on the sidewalk in the cool air for a long time before sitting down on a cold stone step. I watched my breath leave in puffs of white steam.

I felt the nearness of a friend behind me. Miranda's heels snapped sharply on the concrete. She sat next to me and leaned her soft-haired head against mine.

"You know?" she asked.

"I know," I said.

"She's gone?" Miranda asked.

"She's gone," I said.

We sat there a long time, watching for Sola.

"I made Mitch an offer," Miranda said. "For the series."

I looked up at her. Her breath was blue in the yellow light of the streetlights.

"He's agreed to my price," she said. "I know what it's like to be near her, to need to be near her. I'll have them delivered to your place tomorrow."

I said nothing, for I had nothing to say. Did Miranda understand? Did she know how I was feeling? I needed Sola. Perhaps Miranda did too.

"Thank you, Miranda." The cold was bringing tears to my eyes. "I—"

We sat there in the cold darkness, each calling out in our own silent way. I'd like to believe that Sola heard us calling to her; that she knew we needed her. Sometimes I wonder if Sola calls out to me, trying to summon me to her. I wonder if she knows I'd cross worlds, and worlds within worlds, to be with her. Sometimes I wonder if Sola has someone she can call to her when she is in need.

I looked at Miranda. Miranda looked at me.

"I know," she said. "I know."

13

I walked home through the chilly, windy streets of Chicago, back to Sola's apartment that had been our apartment that was now my apartment. How was I going to explain her absence to our friends and neighbors and the building manager? The plan was to tell everyone that Sola left for home: moved back to Pennsylvania to be closer to her parents, who she'd been missing for some time. The difficulty wouldn't be the lie, or even maintaining the lie: the difficulty would be pretending that Sola was here on Earth, within reach.

The walk was long and winding and much needed. My head throbbed most of the way. Damn headaches seemed to be creeping in frequently now. By the time I reached home it was past midnight.

Inside I stood at the window—the window that Sola had stood before, naked, gorgeous, gazing up at the sky—and watched the stars for a long time, wondering where she was now and who she was tending to. I meandered through the apartment, drifting from room to room; lingering in each, trying to catch a glimpse or a smell of her, hoping to capture whatever essence she'd left behind for me. The rooms held only emptiness.

I'd saved the bedroom for last, not wanting to face the empty bed.

She had always been with me; I'd never slept here alone.

When I pushed the bedroom door open, I left the light off. I shut my eyes tight and stepped inside, returning for the moment to my life of blindness, that state of being that had shaped my destiny and led me to Sola Pyne. Standing there in the blackness, I focused my attention to my surroundings listening and smelling, relying on the senses that had first brought me to Sola's truth.

Then I heard it. A sound I had forgotten about over the past few months: the buzzing of bees. A distant humming hidden in the darkness of the room.

Eyes shut tight, I breathed deeply and, though it was faint, smelled the tell-tale scents of alcohol, saltwater and burning hair. I followed the sound to Sola's closet and pulled open the doors. Pushing my hands into her clothes, I traced the length of garment toward the floor until at last, my hands touched the slightly rounded lid of the cold, metal chest.

Only once had I opened this box, and that had terrified me. Now I was not afraid, but curious. What was the inside like? In the pictures Bloirngik had been huge. How big was the space within this chest?

Only one way to know.

I stepped one foot inside, feeling for a bottom. When I found a solid purchase, I was disappointed, but pressed on. I wasn't willing to give her up yet. There had to part of Sola left in this place. I climbed in with both feet, sat down inside, and pulled the lid shut on me.

Wind rushed past me as I floated - or fell, maybe - through a void. I was tempted to open my eyes, but didn't. In that moment, in the rush of sinking into that other world, I was more comfortable in blindness. Let me experience this new world the way I lived in mine, I thought. The scent of ocean was strong now, overwhelming all other smells. The sound of crashing waves broke through the roar of the wind.

Then I was sitting on sand. I don't remember landing or crashing. There was no sudden stop at the end of the fall. I was in the air, then I was on the ground. The sand was hot and course in the palms of my hands. I had travelled, as Sola does, to a world other than my own.

Standing, I opened my eyes and looked at my surroundings.

The land was barren. Only sandy beach to the horizon in every direction except on my left. That was ocean: a vast body of water the color of Sola's flesh. I desired to write a message to Sola, put it in a bottle, then throw it out into the sea, but I had no paper or bottle. But what message would I have sent at that point? Maybe just, *I still need you.*

I walked along that beach, eyes open wide, no longer relying on the crutch of my blindness. That crutch, my ailment of blindness, had been a necessary affliction for the healing of my mind, for without my blindness I don't believe Sola could have taught me to see. But now I had this gift of sight that she'd given to me with her extraordinary gift and I was going to use my new sight, and my new vision, gratefully.

After I'd walked long enough to believe I was on an island and would never run out of shoreline, I saw a great mound in the distance, rising out of the water. I knew what it was the moment my eyes fell on it: the gigantic corpse of Bloirngik. He was everything that Mitch Lovecraft painted him to be. From the squid-face to the tentacle-limbed bottom half. I didn't get very close; I couldn't. Something more magnificent than this alien creature stood between his carcass and me.

Having repaired his damaged body, sustained him, and then killed him, Sola's bacteria had streamed out of Bloirngik's body. Their purpose served, the tiny creatures teemed upon the beach, swaying to a fro like wheat in wind, as if searching for something to infest, to heal; but here in Bloirngik's hospice world there were no living creatures, only them and me, and I was not in need of their aid. Time must work differently in this containment device that housed Bloirngik in his final days. It had been a few months in my world since Sola had told me that Bloirngik had died, but here he was before me, apparently not yet starting to decay. And I thought the bacteria would die when the host died, but the carpet of creatures squirming from the massive corpse streamed toward the ocean. Were they going out to sea to die?

It came then, the final headache. I thought for sure this one would kill me. Pain overcoming me, I collapsed to the sand, resigned to die on this beach, under the pink sky, in Bloirngik's shadow. I lay back on the sand only to realize that it was not sand; I had lain on the writhing field of the bacteria. They were glad to have me. A buzzing welled within my brain, a song that was taken up all around me by the billions of bacteria as they carried me out onto that vast blue sea.

Lights flashed in the sky and I thought I saw Sola's face, thought I felt the cool, electric touch of her hand on my face. I was happy, at peace. As I drifted out on that living raft, I drifted into sleep: a sleep I'd thought to be my last.

I awoke some time later on the bedroom floor, next to Sola's closet, next to the chest. That day I packed all of her clothes and belongings, the things she would have taken if she had really moved back to Pennsylvania, into the chest. Then I threw the chest into Lake Michigan. I had no need of it. There was nothing left inside for me.

14

The following Friday the delivery men came.

They brought the half-dozen paintings comprising "The Rescue of the Traveler Out of Time." Miranda paid handsomely for this series, I have no doubt, and will forever be in her debt. Miranda had sent a letter with the men, asking me to let them take the small statuette of Sola that had fallen on me the day of Lovecraft's showing. I had told her about that night, as we set on the step outside the gallery. In its place the men left me a check from Miranda with a figure large enough that I could take a month off.

I set the series up in order, in a semi-circle near the window where Sola was wont to stand during the dark hours, watching the sky. I spend many days sitting before these paintings, watching her move from one to the next. I know that she's out there now, moving from life to life, healing and bringing peace to those who need it. Sola said that humans suffer abundantly and she has spent much time on Earth. As I watch the paintings and the sky beyond them, I wait for the day when Sola Pyne is summoned back to Earth. Perhaps she will wander back into my life. I'll stay here, in this apartment, sculpting, painting, living, and waiting for her. If she does come back, she'll know where to find me. Of course, I could go anywhere and she'd find me. I just have to whisper into the dark of night, and Sola will hear my voice. But will a whisper of a healthy man be enough to call her back to me?

Yes, I'm healthy. I always will be, until the end. Sola's power remains within me, dwelling in the creatures she left behind; they will be a part of me until the end, as will she.

Though the bacteria remain, I don't have headaches so much anymore; not unless I'm thinking about the truth of the universe or of the world or of worlds within worlds. But those headaches are something altogether different.

Rhett Craig Bruno

Hailing from White Plains, New York, Rhett's been writing for as long as he can remember. While studying architecture at Syracuse University he continued to write. Then, as a senior, he decided to pursue his passion for Science Fiction. Currently working as an architect, he continues to work on ideas that bounce around inside his head. His most recent publication is Perihelion SF short story titled "This Long Vigil." Look for his upcoming novel, *Titanborn*, due out in 2016.

The Far Side of Psyche

"Gav!" Sybil hollered, snapping her fingers in front of Gavin Flynn's face. She didn't have to reach very far. Even though its crew only consisted of two people, the cockpit of the *Columbus* was cramped. "Gav, wake up."

"Huh?" Gavin blinked open his eyes to see the speckled, black canvas of space stretching infinitely before him. Staring out through the ship's viewport had apparently caused him to dose off.

How long was I out? He swept his gaze down to the ship's control console positioned between him and Sybil. His finger tapped the screen and he sifted through data until he pulled up their coordinates. His heart sank when he discovered the answer. They'd passed the Yerkhov Band barely five minutes earlier.

"Yup, you missed it," Sybil said. "I tried to wake

you, but I guess you really needed the rest. Top-of-the-line, Trion Corp sleep-pods and you haven't spent more than a day in one since we set off from Luna." She gestured behind them to the two glassy slots set on either side the passageway which attached to the rest of the *Columbus*.

Gavin rubbed his eyes and sat up straight. "Would you mind if we looped around and crossed it again?" he asked. At first he thought he was making a joke, but upon further consideration he realized he wouldn't mind.

The Yerkhov Band represented the furthest distance outward from Earth that a manned ship had ever knowingly ventured. In 2024 AD, famed Soviet explorer Dimitri Yerkhov reached the point while on a bold expedition to Saturn, but allegedly had to turn back due to a life-support malfunction. Afterward his nation claimed that Yerkhov retired into shameful solitude on the red planet, but Gavin was part of the small party which knew that was a lie. In truth, the ship never got a chance to turn around. An unexplained catastrophe caused its engines to overload, boiling Yerkhov and his small crew alive.

That occurred only a year and a half before Gavin and Sybil set off on their current mission, but even a year in the seemingly interminable space race between the United States and the USSR could seem like an eternity. When the States placed their first mining station on the Moon in 2008, Mars was a distant dream. Now, the Soviets were busy constructing the first domed city on its ruddy surface.

"Trust me, you didn't miss anything," Sybil said. "Just blackness all around us like everywhere else." She placed her hand gently upon Gavin's shoulder. He

112

didn't look over, but felt a few strands of her curly blonde hair rub against his neck. They were soft as silk. "You really shouldn't spend so much time up here, Gav," she added, her lips twisted with concern.

"You don't ever like to stare out and wonder what could possibly be around all those stars?"

"When you know every single constellation by heart, and remember exactly where you were the first time you saw each one, you try not to think of them much. It can be exhausting."

"Right," Gavin chuckled. "I forgot about your memory." He sighed. "I don't know, maybe you're right. I just can't help it."

"I'm always right," she said. "What was it your dad said? 'Staring out into space for too long will drive a man mad'?"

"Bah, he was just bitter! I swear, before the damn Soviets planted their red flag on the red planet, he found it just as spectacular as I do."

"Well wouldn't he be delighted then, now that we're officially farther from Earth than any human before us."

As usual, she was right. Yerkhov was Gavin's father's chief rival in space, and surpassing his mark should've been a prize in itself. Gavin, however, had a hard time being proud of crossing what had become a constant reminder of exactly how perilous the unknown could be. He instead found himself more relieved. There was a prevalent belief amongst the people who knew about Yerkhov's fate that there existed some manner of fatal, cosmic anomaly along the Yerkhov Band. Gavin had little doubt it was just superstition, but a small part of him wanted to be ready for anything just in case. He felt foolish that by pushing himself to his limits he napped straight through it.

"It's about time," Gavin declared, deciding to force a smile for Sybil's sake as he did. "Now we'll mark a new line when we finally reach Psyche."

Sybil rolled her eyes. "You really are his son. Can't you just enjoy the moment for once?"

"Sorry… Maybe those Soviet bastards will finally stop patting themselves on the back for beating us to Mars!" He hollered triumphantly. "That better?"

"Much!" She let her hand slide down his arm and come to rest on top of his. It was all he could manage not to blush as he angled his head in her direction. She was staring straight into his eyes. "It really is beautiful though, Gav. I hope you know how proud he is."

"I know. It's hard for him after losing out on Mars, but I know he never truly lost his love for being out here. It's in our blood."

Out of the corner of his eye, Gavin noticed the picture of his father, Charles Flynn, pinned to edge of the *Columbus'* viewport. It was an old Polaroid which his mother took before one of his earlier missions. His spacesuit had an American flag sewn to the chest that was so dated it only had fifty stars, but what Gavin always focused on was the fact he was smiling.

His father had dedicated his life to planning the first manned mission to Mars, until the Soviets beat him to it. He was never the same after that lone failure, despite being one of the finest cosmonauts the United States had known since the first moon landing. It caused him to give up on what he loved, but for Gavin, who lived to make him proud, the Space Race chugged on. The USA had the moon, the Soviets got Mars, and now Gavin was after the next holy grail of inter-solar exploration. The *Columbus,* his own life's work, was being sent to intercept the most metal-rich asteroid in the main belt – Psyche – and send it hurtling back to Earth using the mobile, Plasmatic Pulse Drives he'd invented.

"Well, when we get back I'll make sure not to tell him you slept through the moment we surpassed the man who stole Mars," Sybil said. "Some great cosmonaut you are!" She nudged Gavin in the side, but before he could retaliate she'd already yanked herself up from her seat and fled the cockpit.

Gavin couldn't help but smirk. He and Sybil had worked together for so long that they were like siblings. Even if deep down he knew he didn't want just that, she was the closest friend he had within the ever-growing extents of human civilization.

"Yeah, if I don't space you by then!" Gavin shouted as he undid his restraints and pulled away from the stars in order to follow her. He pushed off the back of his seat and drifted into the galley where he found Sybil hovering next to the food bin. She was holding a Trion-Corp Ration Bar in either hand, and wore a goofy grin like she'd just discovered the wheel.

"A special dinner is in order," she announced, as if presenting to a crowd. "What'll it be, Mac and cheese flavor, or wait, chicken soup."

"Hmm, they're both classics," Gavin chuckled. "Hell, the food is half the reason I signed up for this."

"I vote for chicken soup, if you don't mind."

Gavin shrugged. "Works for me."

She handed over one of the bars and motioned for him to join her at their makeshift table. It was little more than the lid of a storage bin strapped on top of some other empty crates, but the overhang was enough to keep their bodies pinned down in zero-g. The

Columbus wasn't built for comfort. Most of its load consisted of hauling three Plasmatic Pulse Drives on the underside.

Sybil raised her Trion-Bar. "To going further than anyone before."

"And hoping that the Soviets never get a chance to see what we're about to see," Gavin added.

"I can toast to that."

They each took a bite. Sybil wore a face of revulsion as she chewed, like she always did while she ate a Trion-Bar. Gavin quickly swallowed his so he could take another bite. After naturally sleeping for so long he was starving, and he honestly didn't mind them. They were packed with all the nutrients the body needed, and as far as he was concerned, some of the flavors actually did taste a bit like their counterparts. Sometimes he'd close his eyes and pretend he was eating the real thing, although the yeasty texture often made it difficult to maintain the illusion.

"How many generations of Flynn's do you think will wind up eating this garbage every day?" Sybil asked after she was finally able to force the first bite down her throat.

"At this point, who knows? Unless I find someone to have children sometime soon, I'm the last able-bodied one left…" Gavin wished he could take back the words as soon as they left his lips.

Sybil very nearly choked on her second, reluctant mouthful of her Trion-Bar. She glared up at him for a moment, her brow furrowed, before deciding to leave it alone and focus on her meal. Gavin was content to do the same. So they sat in silence, eating the first meal for any human on the other side of where Dimitri Yerkhov was blown to bits.

Before either of them could finish, a continuous beeping sounded throughout the galley. It wasn't the emergency alarm, but it was enough to make Gavin's eyes go wide. He shoved off from the counter and used the ceiling bars to heave himself back into the cockpit.

"What is that?" Sybil asked. She followed close behind.

"Proximity alert for Psyche," Gavin answered.

"That doesn't make any sense. We're still days out of its orbit trajectory according to what the scanners said last week."

"I know."

Gavin slid his weightless body into his seat and strapped in. He didn't think there was anything hazardous to worry about, but it'd become a manner of habit. He swiped his hand across the control console and saw the alert was correct. Since passing by Mars' orbit there'd been nothing but the green blip of the *Columbus* floating in the center of the three-dimensional navigation array, with countless coordinate lines tracing across the blackness. Now there was another mark, and according to the data their scanners had gathered it was definitely Psyche. The size and mass were a perfect match, as well as the readout of its basic, metallic composition.

"That's definitely it," Gavin said. "I'm trying to see why the scanners didn't pick anything up until now, but there seems to be interference from Psyche's magnetic field or something." His heart was beginning to race in excitement. Again and again he read through all of the data popping up on the screen to make sure he wasn't missing something.

Sybil strapped in beside him. "Did we miscalculate our speed?"

"Nope, holding steady at 16.0 Kilometers per second. Another asteroid must've collided with it and altered its orbit." He laughed and looked at Sybil, beaming. "Are you ready?"

She didn't appear anywhere near as pleased as she took over at the control console and scrolled through the data to try and get a clearer picture. "I… it just doesn't make any sense. Sure a collision is technically possible, but I don't think it'd be so drastic."

"A lot can happen in a week at these speeds. It could've been scraps drifting out from the construction efforts on Mars as well. We'll figure that out later, for now we've got a rock to catch. Ready thrusters."

Sybil exhaled slowly before she reached up and flipped a few of the switches above her head. Red lights strung along the edges of the viewport flashed on and the straps on their chests tightened. Then the gelatinous surface of their seats loosened and began forming around the cambers of their backs.

"Thrusters ready," Sybil replied. Gavin could tell she was nervous, but they'd been working together for so long that he had her complete trust. It was why he'd never choose anyone else to serve as his partner.

"Psyche is approaching from our portside at 17.5 kilometers per second," Gavin said. "Just a brief, max-burn to match velocity. Do you think you'll be able to make the turn on such short notice without killing us?"

Even with the seat forming a snug shell around the back of her head she managed to put on the most self-assured sneer Gavin had ever seen. "No problem. You just leave the piloting to me."

"Works for me. You have the intercept course down?"

She poured over the information on the control

console for a few seconds before nodding. "On your mark, captain."

"Engaged."

Gavin punched the ignition key then clutched the arms of his chair hard enough to turn his knuckles white. The *Columbus'* main rocket-thrusters flared on, propelling the ship so fast the countless conduits threading its interior corridors rattled against the walls. Tremendous pressure built up around his chest. The force radiated across his entire body until it felt like he was being crushed between two faces of a massive vice. Without the malleable seat bracing him it would've been enough to snap his back in two.

The stress building behind his eyes made it impossible open them, but he didn't have to. Sybil was the best pilot in the States and because of her eidetic memory she'd already memorized the path they needed to take before they went on their burn. There was no time to have bothered programming it into the computer if they wanted to keep pace with Psyche. He could hear the tips of her nails confidently tracing the *Columbus'* path across her seats control panel.

"We're coming up to 17.5 now," Sybil groaned through her clenched teeth. "Altering course in three, two, one…"

Here we go dad. One small step.

All of a sudden Gavin felt his insides slam into the left side of his rib cage. The ship banked hard to the right, on an arc so tight that he thought he was going to vomit. It didn't last long, and when they straightened out everything inside him seemed to fall right back into their proper places. The weight on his chest vanished as swiftly as it arrived, leaving his body as achy as it would've been had he just run a marathon. The straps over his chest loosened and the gelatinous surface of the seat returned to its static position.

He opened his eyes. Sybil was already gawking through the viewport at the bulbous gray figure of Psyche now above them. It and the ship's speeds were synchronized, and it almost appeared like they weren't moving at all. The stars, however, edged by ever so sluggishly to remind Gavin they were.

"Whew! We're on pace," she stuttered, clearly forgetting to breathe before she started speaking.

They turned to each other and locked gazes. Both had tears welling in the corners of their eyes. Gavin grabbed her by the arm and shook it excitedly. He always had reservations when it came to touching her, but his own insecurities seemed trivial in the face of Psyche. Its craterous exterior harbored more valuable metals then Earth had wielded even before humans carved up its surface.

"We're here," Gavin said. "Look at it Sybil. I wonder if the president will think the billions were worth it now."

"We'll ask him as soon as we get this rock back." She leaned forward in her seat and perched over the piloting controls like a hawk searching for prey. "Shall we begin?"

"Whenever you're ready. Get us close enough to the far side and we'll begin planting the Pulse Drives in their assigned coordinates."

"Simple enough. One problem though. The drives were programmed for where Psyche was *supposed* to be."

"Right… Leave that to me." Gavin began rifling through data on the control console.

Sybil may have been the pilot, but this was his

area of expertise. He created the Plasmatic Pulse Drives after all. They utilized supercritical fusion pulses for propulsion so they were still too volatile to be used on occupied ships, but an asteroid was different. After they were activated, Psyche was supposed to reach Earth's orbit in less than a month. The three drives were to be set at equal intervals along one hemisphere of the asteroid, and once it was close enough they were programmed to spin the asteroid 180 degrees. They'd fire back in the other direction, slowing Psyche down enough so that it gently tapped into the moon without causing any real damage and could be trapped. That was the plan, as long as Gavin hadn't miscalculated anything.

"I'm recalibrating based on the new orbit," he said. "It shouldn't take too long. We're only a few million miles off the mark."

"That's all?" Sybil quipped.

Gavin grinned and continued his work. The *Columbus* began to rise gradually toward the asteroid as he did. The forward viewport wrapped up over their heads, so Psyche was visible even as they got closer.

"Hey Gav, what's that?" Sybil asked.

"What's what?" He didn't bother to look up.

"There's something clinging to the asteroid."

Gavin's finger slipped off the screen. He glared up and followed the line of her pointing finger toward what she was talking about. The shell of what looked like a ship floated alongside the far side of Psyche beside a cluster of scrap-metal. Some more of it stuck to the surface, bunched around a charred patch of rock contrasting with the asteroid's mostly gray coloration. There was a string of red streaks along the hull, and on one of them it looked like…

"Is that a Soviet Flag?" Gavin mouthed. He immediately assumed the worst. That like his father before him, the Soviets had stolen his research, and beat him to his mark.

"I'm going to try to get closer," Sybil said. "We're going to need a little juice, hold on."

The straps on Gavin's chest stiffened and his seat began to shape to his body again before they shot forward. The rate of acceleration was low enough for him to keep his eyes open this time, so he squinted to try and get a better idea of what they were seeing. It was a Soviet Flag alright, even though half of the hammer and sickle emblem was burned. Beneath it there was a patch of Russian text. He couldn't read it, but he'd seen it in thousands of photographs.

"Sybil…That's Yerkhov's ship-"

A blinding flash painted the region in front of the viewport white. It made his eyes sting, and as soon as he averted his gaze whatever had produced it tore into the hull of the *Columbus*. The ship was hewed in half, as easily as a child snapping a cheap plastic toy. A powerful rush of air promptly followed, pulling at Gavin's cheeks and pinning him to his seat. The deafening howl was squelched by space in an instant. The only thing that saved him and Sybil from being yanked out by the rapid change in pressure as well was that they were restrained.

Countless emergency protocol sessions and seminars allowed Gavin to keep his wits about him while the *Columbus* tumbled through space and the looser parts of the cockpit zipped by his head. Survival instincts kicked in. He did the first thing that came to mind and held his breath. The life support systems in the cockpit were draining fast and once they were exhausted just inhaling could cause his lungs to collapse.

He then snatched two helmets out of the storage cabinet at his side. Its doors had already been ripped off, but luckily they were strapped down.

He placed one over Sybil's head first. She was either in shock or had passed out because she didn't move. Once she was secured he lifted the other and snapped it into place on the collar of his own space-suit. Again, Gavin was relieved that he tried to always stick to protocol. The Academy recommended for the crew of any spacefaring vessel to be in their space-worthy suits whenever they weren't in sleep pods.

An airtight seal formed around his neck with a soft hiss, allowing fresh air to flow in through the reserves woven into his suit. He gratefully guzzled down a mouthful. There was at least three hours' worth of oxygen available if he was careful.

Once Gavin was able to focus he heard Sybil panting uncontrollably through the two-way com-link built into their helmets. "Are you okay?" he asked. "Can you breathe?"

He reached out, clutched her hand and squeezed. Seeing her in that state had his heart thumping against his chest so fast that it hurt. *Stay calm. Focus.*

"What the fuck was that," she gasped.

Gavin's response got lost in his throat. There was little doubt who it was. The solar system wasn't yet filled with space pirates the likes of which littered the pages of the science fiction stories he'd grown up reading. Yerkhov's death was just another lie. He and the Soviets had beaten them to Psyche and shot down the *Columbus* to keep the secret. The flash which preceded the blast ruled out it being any ordinary shred of debris.

Gavin turned his attention away from Sybil for a

moment and studied the ship's control console. The air pressure in the cockpit – or lack of it – had regulated by then, allowing him to lean forward and check the damage report. Somehow the majority of the cockpit and the bundle of Pulse Drives attached to its undercarriage were left intact. That was the least of his concerns, however. The blast had sent him, Sybil, and what remained of the *Columbus* bowling toward the rocky surface of the asteroid with no means of braking.

He glanced up at the viewport. They were spinning so fast that it made him dizzy to look for more than a few seconds. Upon every rotation he could see the silvered remnants of the rear portion of the *Columbus* fraying into the blackness, the great vacuum squelching any flames like fingers squeezing a lit candle.

When he was finally able to respond, he yelled, "The Soviets have gone too far this time!"

"How could they know we were headed here?" Sybil questioned.

Gavin's fingers began to go numb from her squeezing them. It was a welcome distraction from how nauseous the spinning was making him. He felt like he was back at the first day of training in the academy.

"Someone planted in NASA, maybe," he said. "I don't know… But there'll be actual fighting over this." The bitter rivalry between Earth's only superpowers had remained without direct altercation ever since Gavin was a child, but an attack on a million-dollar vessel carrying billion-dollar prototype Plasmatic Pulse Drives was likely to change that. The greater solar-system was ripe with plenty of desirable resources that both factions craved passionately.

"Tell them we're unarmed then and to stand down!" Sybil yelled.

"I'd love to, but they're the least of our problems right now." Gavin looked back up and saw the unforgiving surface of Psyche growing steadily nearer before the *Columbus* flipped around once more and gave him a view of the stars. "These seats might survive the crash, but I doubt we will."

Sybil examined the ship's control console for herself. Gavin couldn't see her face through the side of her helmet, but he could hear the heartbreak in her tone as she said, "We've lost both engines and the bow thrusters won't respond."

"I know. Just breathe," Gavin whispered calmly to her before taking his own advice. He had to remain the poised one, for her sake. If he could convince the government that a mission to literally grab an asteroid was necessary, then he could manage to stop his fragmented ship before they were squashed like insects. Solving problems was one thing he was good at.

No engines. He closed his eyes so he wouldn't see their impending doom and allowed his mind to race back through countless hours of training and research. Unexpectedly, he found his answer in one of his first lessons. He remembered one night with his dad, on their farm out in Wisconsin, where the stars shone bright. They were shooting at bottles, and he was hardly big enough to hold the rifle. The first time he fired the gun the recoil sent him flying back onto his rear. He could still hear the hearty laughter of his dad as well as the words he'd said right after. *For every action.* That was it.

"You see those controls?" Gavin gestured excitedly to a series of dials located on the console above Sybil's head. "When I say, turn them. They each release a Pulse Drive. Wait until they're facing the asteroid, then we'll fire them off to soften our impact. At this angle we should bounce off cleanly.... Relatively. Can you do that?"

She didn't say anything.

"Sybil, I can't see your head," Gavin said. "No nodding, alright?"

"Right, sorry," she said. "Don't we risk losing them if they aren't set down properly?"

That part of the equation hadn't entered Gavin's mind. If he was alone he probably would've stopped right then and there and set them to overload instead. It would no doubt kill him, but at least the Soviets would never get a hand on his prototype. Only he wasn't alone. He could see the pale reflection of Sybil's terrified face in the viewport, her lips quivering and her cheeks stained with tears. Beyond it, Psyche was so close that every time the *Columbus* spun toward the rockbound landscape filled the entire view.

Time was running out.

"We'll figure that out after," Gavin decided. "Just do it!"

"O... Okay."

"Remember, there are three so you're going to have to be quick. I'm going to start counting down from five now." Gavin paused to get a better idea of their rotation speed, and then waited until just the right moment to start his countdown.

"Five... four... three... two... one... Now!"

Sybil's hands fluttered across the dials. The *Columbus* lurched three times successively, and right after the last jump the top of it banged into the surface of the asteroid. Gavin and Sybil's bodies were launched forward, but the straps on their seats caught them. A thin crack zigzagged across the outer layer of the viewport's glass, but not deep enough to break it.

Gavin released the mouthful of air he hadn't even realized he was holding. The gravity of the asteroid was weak enough to allow the *Columbus* to bounce back a short distance before it wound up caught in its orbit. He unstrapped himself so he could peer back over his shoulder and finally get a visual of the damage they'd sustained.

All that remained of the galley were the jagged ends of broken structure framing the blackness of space. He watched with a heavy heart as the three Plasmatic Pulse Drives also knocked into the asteroid and rebounded to follow them in orbit. The claw-like, landing gear at the base of their metal-plated, cylindrical casings snapped off like twigs.

For a moment, Gavin forgot everything else. They were his most significant gift to humanity, with the possibility of one day allowing realistic inter-solar travel, and now they were floating aimlessly for anyone to grab.

"Mayday, mayday!" He heard Sybil shout through their com-link, freeing him from his stupor. "This is the research vessel, *Columbus,* of the United States of the Americas. We are unarmed!"

Gavin turned to see her leaning over the ship's central console. She was trying to sync the *Columbus'* systems to her helmet's com-link so she could send out a broad transmission on all known frequencies.

"Mayday, mayday!" she yelled, louder this time. "I repeat, this is a research vessel carrying prototype engines and we are unarmed!" There were a few seconds of silence, and then she slammed the console with her fist. "Damn, Nothing!"

"Let me look." Gavin propped himself up and

brushed her aside. The console's screen flickered, and the ghosts of outlandish characters had begun popping up in place of the English text. They didn't appear Russian. "Something's jamming us," he said. "If this is Soviet, it's new tech. The computer isn't down, but all transmissions are bouncing right back to us as if we're stuck in a cocoon."

"Can you fix it?"

His fingers danced across the screen, but the further into the system he delved, the more alien the programming he'd designed became. "I don't know," he grumbled. "I'll need time to crack it. I just don't know how much."

"Well they haven't fired again, yet," Sybil said. "That must mean something."

"Maybe they think we're dead." He placed one of his hands upon her shoulder, and even through her suit he could feel her whole body trembling. "They won't get away with this, Syb. Whatever happens, someone will find out what they've done and they'll pay."

Before Gavin could answer, the ship jolted upwards. He braced himself for another blast, but none came.

"Did you do that?" Sybil asked.

"I don't think so," Gavin said. The screen of the control console went completely black for a moment before being replaced by green static. He tapped it a few times, but it didn't change.

"Gavin?"

He lifted off of his seat and crawled along the cockpit's ceiling, which at some point had become his floor. He kept going until he reached the end of what was left of the corridor, exited the cockpit, and pulled himself up to peer around the frazzled edge.

"What the…" he mouthed. The hairs on the back of his neck stood on end. They were approaching a gigantic, purplish blur in space. It had a bulbous shape, and a palpable stream of energy radiated outward from it which distorted the stars beyond.

"Gavin, what is it?" Sybil asked.

He poked his body out further to get a better look. The blur was getting closer and closer, and only when he looked down did he realize they were actually getting further away from Psyche and slowly drawn towards whatever *it* was. That was when he also realized the side of the asteroid the *Columbus* was now facing had four giant rings of reddish lights along the wrinkled surface which definitely weren't natural.

"I have no idea," Gavin said.

Sybil appeared next to him and took a look as well. Through her visor he saw her mouth drop open. Before he knew what was happening she was clutching him, closer than she'd ever been to him before. Any other time he would've reveled in the moment, but all he could think about was he wished he'd left her behind. Whatever they'd stumbled upon, there was a feeling growing in the depths of his mind that it had nothing to do with Yerkhov or the Soviets.

"I don't think that's Soviet," Sybil pronounced, as if reading Gavin's mind.

"I don't think that's… human," he whispered.

Gavin couldn't believe what he'd just said. It was ridiculous. Yet the further they rose, the more he was sure he'd never seen anything similar. The blur was like an illusion. If he switched his angle of vision it became a distorted blob of stars, as if it were mirroring them in an attempt to camouflage.

Suddenly, a portion of space folded inwards,

revealing a chamber flooded with dim, crimson light. The architecture inside was unrecognizable. Thick, sweeping metallic arches held up an undulating ceiling so it looked like they were entering into the rib cage of a gargantuan beast.

"That's insane," Sybil snapped. "You're insane." She backed off of him and stumbled against the wall of the ruptured corridor. "No, this is impossible."

Gavin opened his mouth to respond, but he was speechless. Even with all of Earth's remarkable telescopes and far-reaching probes, neither his people nor the Soviets had ever detected any genuine signs of life, especially running amuck in their own solar system. And then he remembered how Dimitri Yerkhov died with no explanation, and the murmurs of anomalies which came with it. In his heart he knew, he was staring at that anomaly. Yerkhov's engines didn't malfunction. They were blasted by something as interested in the asteroid belt as humans were.

"What do we do?" Sybil asked. "They shot the *Columbus* down without as much as a warning. If that is, whatever you think it is, which it isn't, then they clearly have no desire to negotiate. If it's not, then whatever faction is behind this will be trying to keep it quiet."

There was no question she was right. Friendly neighbors don't fire across the street just to say hello. Of all the possible issues Gavin had considered while he was planning the Psyche mission, this was one that never came up. The explorer in him was overwrought with questions about what the discovery meant, but the loving friend in him knew if they didn't find a way off the *Columbus* they were going to join Yerkhov in infamy and nobody would ever find out the truth. Every second they wasted, the strange, hellish room was getting closer, like a blooming red rose upon a sheet of black silk. Gavin racked his brain for answers, but there were none.

"Look!" Sybil was leaning far out through the severed end of the *Columbus* and pointing beneath them. "The drives are rising too."

Gavin looked. The trio of Plasmatic Pulse Drives were beneath them, twisting around each other as they climbed the stars. Two of them were heavily damaged, but the last one to smack into Psyche appeared intact. With the landing gear broken off, they appeared like little more than unassuming metal tubes with long exhaust vents running along the shafts and fins on either end. Within those tubes, however, the fastest engines known to man were cradled.

Thanks to Sybil, the beginnings of a plan began hatching in Gavin's mind. He'd always known he built the Plasmatic Pulse Drives for a reason. Until then, he'd just assumed they were for the wrong one.

"Sybil, which way are we facing?" he asked.

"Facing?" she said. "I don't know what you mean."

"In Sol! I know you've memorized the stars, so which one of them is actually Mars. Whatever we're heading towards, we shouldn't be around to face it."

Sybil immediately began naming off star constellations under her breathe. "There!" she shouted after a few seconds and gestured to one of the stars which was even bright through the distortion field.

"Don't lose it," Gavin said.

"Why? What're you up to, Gavin, we don't have much time!"

"We're going to hitch a ride in one of the Pulse Drives straight to the red planet."

"You're going to give your work to the Soviets?" she countered, completely in shock.

"I'm not giving them anything. Something's out here and we need to tell someone. Soviet or American, Mars is the only settled place close enough to reach without suffocating first."

Gavin pulled himself back down the corridor and stopped at the portion of the wall where Sybil's sleep-pod was built in, right outside the cockpit proper. It was only a few meters away from where the Columbus snapped, but somehow it hadn't been comprised. He popped open the lid and turned back to her.

"Get in," he ordered. "With the computers corrupted we won't be able to signal the Pulse Drives from here, but I can activate them on manually. I'll drag you down to one, fire it up, and hop in with you. We'll hitch a ride straight to Mars."

"We'll have better luck inside of whatever that thing is!" Sybil countered. "You said it yourself; they aren't ready for ship-use yet. The radiation will be too much. I'd rather be probed than microwaved."

"The fusion reactions are focused externally, but the pod's small enough to fit inside the casing. Trion builds them dense enough to withstand extreme conditions, and it's got enough oxygen stores built-in to last the trip. You'll make it"

He watched as Sybil gaped up into the maw of the unknown, then back at him. Judging by her pained expression he knew that for the first time she didn't have complete faith in his plan. He wasn't entirely confident in it either, but it was the only way. In a few moments they were going to be entirely inside an alien chamber large enough to fit one hundred *Columbus'* in a straight line.

Sybil took a deep breath before she gave in and started to climb into the pod. She hesitated once she was halfway in. "Gavin, this is crazy," she said. "This can't be what you're thinking. It just can't be. It's the Soviets playing a trick on us so they can steal your work."

Gavin knew it wasn't above them to craft an elaborate scheme like this just to get away with stealing valuable technology, but he doubted it. "If it is, we'll use it to blow a hole in New Moscow when we get there for what they've done," he began. "If it's not, then we'll have made the single greatest discovery in history. I can live with either option. Now get in, strap yourself down and turn on the air just for a few seconds. After I reopen the lid switch it off immediately. We can't waste any oxygen."

Gavin quickly rushed up to the front of the cockpit as she followed his instructions. His father's picture was folded over, but somehow the tape holding it against the viewport hadn't been peeled off entirely. He took it and tucked it into the belt of his suit. By the time he returned to the sleep-pod, the *Columbus* was fully inside of the nightmarish chamber. A darkness more abysmal than space closed in around him, like he was trapped in eternal twilight.

"Air's flowing," Sybil announced.

Gavin keyed the lid of the sleep-pod to open. The rush of air escaping from it caused the entire thing to shoot out from its slot in the wall. It slammed into his side, undoubtedly cracking a rib or two. He held back a scream and ignored the pain as he grappled onto the side of the pod and helped guide it out of the *Columbus*. Once he emerged, he pushed off of the hull of the ship, propelling them down through the opening in the alien chamber's floor and toward the ascending Pulse Drives. The distortion field pulled at the soles of his feet, but it wasn't strong enough to slow him completely.

Sybil's pod glanced harmlessly off of the first Pulse Drive they passed, giving him a chance to kick off again and gather more speed. He was heading for the furthest one which remained in the best shape, but also in hopes to buy as much time as possible.

"Brace yourself, Sybil," he warned once they were closing in. "This is going to be rough."

Her pod smacked into the center of the enormous Pulse Drive's casing. He grabbed onto the service hatch as quickly as he could before they recoiled away. A sharp pain shot up the entire right side of his body, but he gritted his teeth and held on.

There was a key-pad on the side of the tube. He knew the code by heart. It was Sybil's birthday.

He typed it in and the hatch popped open silently, revealing the stagnant core of the drive's reactor. It was the size of a small trailer, but there was plenty of room around it so it could breath. Enough to easily fit one tiny pod. After it was activated, the fusion pulses would be funneled out of one end in order to gain propulsion. Gavin bet Sybil's life on the notion that the Trion Corp constructed sleep-pod would be able to endure the extreme temperatures and radiation leaking around it.

Before climbing in, he glanced up at the area of distorted space. The uppermost Pulse Drive was already being swallowed by the breach, which meant there was no time to waste second guessing.

Weightlessness made it easy to maneuver the sleep-pod so that he could shove the narrow end through the hatch. He positioned it, and then pulled himself toward the top. Sybil was staring anxiously at him through the translucency. Freckles dotted her rosy cheeks, the stars of her own little universe. As he gazed into her watery blue eyes, he knew he was doing what he had to. The stars were impressive, but she was the most beautiful thing in the universe.

"C'mon!" she shouted.

Gavin put on a smile. He reached down and locked the sleep-pod from the outside. They could squeeze in together, but with two of them the air would never last to Mars. He'd figured that out as soon as the plan entered his mind. His Pulse Drives were fast, but they weren't that fast.

"Gav, what are you doing?" Sybil asked.

Gavin breathed in the sight of her for a second or two more. For him it seemed like an eternity. When he was done he shoved the pod down into the open space around the reactor core.

"Gavin, don't!"

He could hear her fists pounding against the inside of the pod through their com-link as she continued to holler his name. He tried to ignore it. There was a control console attached to the reactor and he tugged his way down along a string of thick conduits until he reached it. He wasn't nearly as good a navigator as she was, but he worked through the calculations necessary to set the drive to run for the approximate distance necessary to reach Mars.

"I'm sorry, Sybil," he whispered. "This is one trip we won't be able to make together."

"Gavin, please." She sobbed uncontrollably. "There's room. I'll breathe as slowly as possible, I promise."

"Remember to use up all the oxygen in your suit before you activate the pod."

"Gav…"

"One of us has to make it. If we really aren't alone, somebody needs to know. When you see them, tell the Soviets the race is over."

"Gavin!"

It took all of his courage, but Gavin struck the ignition key. Flashing lights began dancing all throughout the inside of the drive. He hauled his weightless body up toward the Pulse Drive's open hatch, right past Sybil's pod. He paused at it. The core was beginning to heat up so fast that he could feel it through his suit.

"Tell my dad I wish he could've been out here with us," Gavin said as he grabbed onto the rim of the drive's service hatch, hauled himself out, then sealed it behind him. "Tell him, that it's because of him that we survived what Yerkhov couldn't."

Gavin turned his head to locate Mars again, and then pushed off of the Pulse Drive's casing with his feet hard enough to tilt it so the nose faced the Soviet-run planet. Once he was away, he was instantly caught in the distortion field. It made his body tingle. He hovered their quietly, trying not to listen as Sybil cried. He watched a bright, cobalt luminance begin to gather on one end of the drive.

"Please… don't… do… this," Sybil whimpered. With the Pulse Drive powering on their feed began to grow more and more muddled.

"All the time we wasted out here together, Sybil, it was never enough," Gavin said. "I've loved you since the day we met at the academy. I hope you know that"

"Gavin, I'm begging you to come –" By the time

those last words came out her voice was reduced to little more than static.

The area around the Plasmatic Pulse Drive grew as bright and blinding as the sun, and then it bolted forward through the alien distortion field. It raced across the blackness like a comet, a trail of blues sparkling in its wake. Gavin had only ever seen it operate in test environments. It was majestic, and as it merged with the rest of the stars the bottom of the hellish chamber closed beneath him.

He found himself lying on a strange floor, surrounded by an oppressive, dusk-like darkness on all sides. Before anything else, he noticed that for the first time in months weight was returning to his body. His limbs were so weak that he could barely lift them and when he tried to get up the pain in his side was too unbearable. He fell back down, groaning in agony into his helmet where nobody in the universe could hear him.

Once the pain subsided enough for him to open his eyes he squinted ahead to see the cloven remnant of the *Columbus* sitting nearby, with the two other Pulse Drives on either side. His stomach turned over when he noticed a silhouette lurking about inside of the ship. It was tall; taller than any human he'd ever seen. There was a mess of hair falling from its head like clumped dreadlocks. Or maybe they were tentacles.

He thought about taking his helmet off to yell out, but he had no idea what the composition of the surrounding air was. He was in such a state of shock that he wasn't even sure he'd be able to get the right words out. Everything he said and did from that point on would have to be carefully considered. If what he was looking at wasn't hostile then he could have a chance, a real chance, at changing everything. Yes, it'd shot the *Columbus* down, but wouldn't his own people have done the same if an unidentified ship carrying what could be misconstrued as weapons passed by?

He swallowed hard and began to slide backwards on the floor cautiously. He didn't make it more than an inch before the head of the silhouette snapped around. Eyes with pupils that gleamed like polished amethysts glared in his direction.

That was when he knew beyond a shadow of a doubt that none of what had happened was some elaborate plan concocted by the Soviets. In fact, the very notion of their rivalry just seemed foolish.

He looked into the face of the answer to the question which had plagued humanity since the dawn of rational thought. The space race was over and both sides had lost. It was over since before it even started.

Humanity wasn't alone.

Derrick Boden

He's a recovering software developer who took up writing to kick the habit. Living now in New Orleans, he's lived on four continents and is an avid traveller as well as adventurer. He's a sucker for the simple things in life: food, drink, and good company. Derrick believes Science Fiction is the perfect avenue for exploring the era's dynamic issues against the backdrop of the future.

Blood on the Horizon

The electrode pads pressed cold against Janet's temples. She tugged her helmet tight and hit the power. The connection was shoddy as hell and pounded like a fresh hangover for the first minute. She gritted her teeth and waited it out. The neural oscillators finished their calibrations and the background noise dropped to a dull hiss.

Her vision snapped into focus. Cody stared at her, his giant purple eyes burned like the thrusters of the colony ship. The angoli curled his wet lips back, showing gums.

"Hello, Janet."

Cody's words pounded in her brain. She fumbled with the power gauge until she could think out a coherent response.

"Hi, Cody."

Good, she wasn't speaking the words aloud. It still took some getting used to, even after months of practice.

She glanced over her shoulder, past the cluttered lab to the doors. The deadbolt was locked and a chair leaned against the handle. Probably overkill, with the engineers all in their meeting, but too much was at stake to take chances.

Cody scratched at a snarl of white fur on his chest. "I missed you."

The stress melted from Janet's shoulders like snowpack in midsummer. She smiled. "I missed you too, Cody."

"You look nervous, today. What happened?"

Janet sighed. Cody had always been a keen observer. He probably knew her better than her own husband, but that wasn't saying much. With how much time she'd been spending down here, she was starting to feel more angoli than human.

"They're getting suspicious. Soon I'll have to tell them about our talks."

Cody pushed air through his toothless mouth. It was cute, the way it made his lips flutter all over.

Janet leaned back and admired the big angoli through the bars. He was sitting with his two hind limbs-the biggest ones-crossed beneath him. His middle hands probed his ape-like torso, fingers slipping through tufts of iridescent fur in search of nonexistent bugs. Electrodes laced from the fingers of his forehands, through the bars and into Janet's helmet. He waggled his fingers and his words slipped into her mind like a second thought. "I will talk to them."

Janet smirked at the thought of Shane trying to

make sense of the alien's idioms.

"That'd be one to remember." A second set of cables ran from her helmet back through the bars where they fed beneath a row of fleshy mounds along Cody's forehead. In the wild, that was where another angoli would press its fingertips, transmitting bursts of microwave radiation directly into his neural pathways.

Janet smiled. It was an elegant means of communication. Sure, it lacked the benefit of distance - for that the angoli relied on simple hand gestures. But it was intimate. Sensual, even. Human conversation always felt mundane and clumsy after a turn in the lab.

Cody smacked his wolf-like lips. "How are my people?"

Janet fought the urge to look down the containment hall, where hundreds of angoli vegetated in the darkness. She pursed her lips. Cody knew damn well how his people were.

She leaned forward and grasped the plastic bars. "I'm sorry. I'm doing all I can."

Cody stopped scratching and drew closer until his snout was centimeters from her fingers. His breath was hot against her knuckles. She shivered.

"Are you?"

"I have to be careful. If they find out that I haven't been harvesting your enzymes, we're both shivved. I'm still building a case. I need more tests."

Cody's big eyes flicked away. "Tests suck."

Janet reached between the bars and touched his long snout. She ran her fingers through his face-fur, and he dipped his head. His tufts were soft and warm, unlike the scraggly excuse for a beard Trilo had subjected her to of late. Why couldn't Trilo be more like Cody? Powerful, yet gentle. Clever. Empathetic.

"The tests are the only way I can prove your sentience, set your people free. It beats harvesting."

Cody glared at her, and she drew her hand back. His fingers drifted to the enzyme sac beneath his gut. He looked pregnant, and she'd only stopped harvesting him a few months ago. His sac was almost as large as it had been when the colonists first touched down on the planet three years ago.

She cursed herself. If she'd only recognized their intelligence back then. But without verbal communication or any technological skills, they looked like blissfully simple herbivores. Cattle. God, how wrong she'd been. And now it might be too late. Shane's harvesting mandate was sucking their enzymes- and their intellect-dry, forcing her to rely on these clandestine lab sessions. And with the breakneck pace of the terraforming operation, soon the outside air would be too oxygenated for the angoli to survive in the wild, even if she was able to convince the engineers to cut them loose.

She grimaced. "You'll have to be patient."

Cody planted his middle fists against the bars.

"Patience is waning. Mid-hands are strong."

Another enigmatic angoli idiom. This one didn't sound friendly. She shivered again.

·　·　·

"You wanted to see me?"

Janet tried not to sound impatient, but she still had two more rounds of tests to go and Cody was waiting.

Trilo stroked his chin, further disheveling his facial shag. "It takes the emergency comms to get some face time with my wife these days."

Janet rolled her eyes. "You know I'm busy. The lab-"

Trilo raised a hand and shifted his gaze away. It was another mannerism he'd picked up from all those hours with Shane. It was damned annoying.

She gripped the railing of the observation deck. Beneath them, the habitat bustled. Welding torches shot bursts of sparks across a dozen construction sites, while engineers streamed through the biosphere's airlocks. Outside, past the sweeping curve of transparency, bright green shya fields stretched to the watery horizon. A thousand geysers burst from the shya's vents, propelling vapor ten kilometers into the air.

Near the fields, rows of laser-towers stood with heads drooped down, collecting dust. Early on, they'd run continuously, vaporizing water from the nearby sea to bolster the atmosphere's oxygen content. But once the colonists discovered the shya vents, and how easily they could spike their oxygen output with the addition of the angoli enzyme, the lasers had been rendered obsolete in the terraforming process. West of the lasers, the colony ship stood like a chrome flag of corporate territoriality, towering above Angol's alien landscape.

Trilo watched her. She clenched her jaw. This game was getting old.

He sighed. "You have to shut it down."

Janet shot him a glare. This didn't sound like the usual argument. "What are you talking about?"

"Your project. The tests." Trilo paused. "Shane knows."

Janet whirled. "What? How the hell-"
Trilo looked away. "I don't know."
She stood sputtering. "I can't stop now! Cody's

made too much progress."

"Cody!" Trilo turned red. "For god's sake, you shouldn't be naming them. You know that's only going to make it harder for you."

"He chose it himself."

Trilo expelled air. "Well, in that case."

"The angoli are sentient! Cody's knocking down test after test. He was reading Plato yesterday through the link. Plato!"

Trilo gnawed on his lip. "You still have to shut it down."

Janet clamped her mouth shut. So that was it. She was the idiot. Proof of angoli sentience would muddle up the terraforming project. So they'd just make sure no proof was found.

She looked out across the shya fields where so recently the angoli had romped and played in lazy packs. Back then, the angoli excreted just enough enzymes to stimulate activity from the plants, releasing the correct quantity of oxygen into the atmosphere for their respiratory systems. It was an elegant ecosystem. Until the colonists arrived. Now, with barrels of harvested enzyme spread across the fields daily, the shya worked in overdrive. Their vents pumped oxygen-enriched vapor into the atmosphere by the metric ton. High-speed terraforming, all thanks to an army of captive angoli.

Janet gripped the rail with both hands. "So now the angoli are collateral damage. How did Shane find out, anyway? You're the only person I told."

Now it was Trilo's turn to sputter. "Janet, you're jeopardizing the entire mission! We didn't travel a hundred years in deep freeze for your pet biology project."

"No, it seems we're only here for Shane's manifest destiny-"

"He's a company man. He's doing what's right for Horizon, and for humanity. You know what state the Solar Colonies were in when we left. We need space, and Angol is perfect! We can't squander this opportunity. Shane's wife-"

"Right. His wife." Janet searched the sky for relief. "I've heard that bullshit story a thousand times, about how her death is a symbol of humanity's overpopulation crisis. She's one person! That's all just an excuse for Shane's megalomania. All he wants from me is a synthetic substitute for the enzyme, and I know exactly how much he'll care about the angoli once he's got it. That synthetic will be their death sentence. In another hundred years, the colony ships will come in droves. Shane will be a hero, and Horizon Enterprises will be powerful beyond their dreams. The angoli will be a footnote in the history books of their own planet."

Trilo bit back a response. His gaze shifted behind her. Footsteps clanged against the catwalk, and drew within a few paces. Janet's back went rigid when she heard the loud breathing.

"Shane," she said.

"I hope I'm not interrupting." His chin and cheekbones formed a sharp isosceles triangle, eyes burning with their usual blend of ambition and contempt. He rested a long-fingered hand atop the old comms array.

Trilo stepped forward to mitigate. "We're just wrapping up here."

Janet shot Trilo a glare. Always playing the peacekeeper, even if it meant shutting his own wife down.

Shane's smile looked misplaced on his face. "I've been meaning to speak with you, Janet. But it looks like Trilo has handled it for me. I'm sure you understand our concern. I'll be sending someone by to collect any laboratory equipment not essential to harvesting or enzyme synthesis."

Janet gnashed her teeth.

"I'd be very disappointed to learn of any other deviations from our agenda. The synthetic enzyme project has taken longer than expected, and I can't say I don't harbor some suspicions. I hope you understand how important it will be for both us, and the angoli."

Janet seethed. Yeah, right. Sure, the synthetic enzyme would eliminate their reliance on the angoli. And an unlimited supply of the stuff would grant them cheap and expedient access to all the oxygen locked up kilometers beneath the surface, thanks to the shya's deep roots and unique extraction process. But once the angoli became unnecessary, they'd be little more than an ethics risk, if they proved sentient after all. Protectorate law was clear on matters of sentience protection.

She shrugged. "Science takes time."

Shane leaned closer. "It would be unfortunate if we had to replace you."

Trilo stepped forward and put a hand on Shane's shoulder. He'd apparently heard enough, but so had she. She pushed past both of them and stormed off.

•　　•　　•

"Feel sick," Cody said.

The auxiliary lights washed him in blue, casting shadows across his furry face. He sat slumped on his side. His eyes visibly struggled to maintain their focus on Janet. It had only been three days since she'd resumed harvesting him, and he was already a shell of his former self. She still hadn't been able to isolate the biological reason for it, but it was clear as day how much effect the enzyme harvesting had on angoli intellect and presence.

"I'm sorry." Janet's backup helmet, ill-sized and poorly-constructed, chafed against her forehead. It was the prototype, and a shoddy substitute for her more recent model. But even Trilo didn't know she still had this one, so it had escaped the clutches of Shane's goons. For now.

Cody titled his head. "Funny old hat."

Janet glanced involuntarily at the door lock, then at the auxiliary power console.

"We have to be more careful now, when we talk."

Cody slumped forward, until his leathery cheek rested against the bars. "Soon Cody can't talk. Too dumb."

Janet blinked back the wetness in her eyes. "I know. We're running out of time. We need to finish these tests."

Cody pointed a middle hand at his mouth. "Thirsty."

Janet checked the glucose bag hanging from the ceiling. The nipple was gummed-up, the bag was sucked dry. The transition back to being harvested had done a number on his metabolism.

Cody motioned through the bars to the adjacent cell. Stacks of bulging bags and feed sacks filled the storage area. He cocked his head in silent appeal then pointed at the keycard dangling on the wall. "Always thirsty, all night."

Janet sighed. It was a harmless request; the keycard would only work on the storage cell. "Alright, but just for a few days, until you adjust. And don't drink the reserves dry or Shane will be banging down the door."

Cody blinked. "Shane and Trilo angry with Cody."

Janet bit her lip. Cody had diagnosed her relationship issues weeks ago, and that was before things had got really bad. Should she tell him Trilo wasn't angry with Cody, but with Janet? That there was no untangling the end of one argument from the start of the next? That they hardly had sex anymore, and when they did it felt like rote?

She shook off the thought. "Sometimes, I feel more like one of you, than one of them."

Cody watched her with his big, sleepy eyes. A trail of drool clung to his lower lip.

"I'm so sorry, Cody."

He dropped his head lower. "Comes and goes. Soon, all gone. Like my people. Unless."

"Unless what?"

Cody flicked his gaze across the lab to the door, then back to Janet. His eyes narrowed to slits and lips curled back.

Janet shivered. That was a new facial expression.

Cody blinked and it was gone. "Unless nothing."

•   •   •

Janet brushed past Trilo on her way into Shane's office. He looked ready to say something, but swallowed his words and hustled off, worry creasing his face.

Janet raised an eyebrow. Were they beyond even the point of talking, now?

"Janet." Shane's voice grated into her thoughts.

She strode up to his desk and planted hands on hips. "Somebody better be dead. I was in the middle of-"

Shane raised a hand and looked away. "I suspect you don't understand how important the enzyme is to our terraforming efforts."

Janet rolled her eyes. Another goddamned lecture. Screw him.

"Sure. It's one in a long line of shortcuts you've approved to fast-track the terraforming project. Once you saw how much oxygen you could pull from the shya with the enzyme, you salivated like a teenager in a porn shop."

Shane's jaw muscles twitched. "Our mission is expedient terraforming-"

"You've got all those fancy lasers. Start vaporizing water again!"

"Those methods take time, and a surplus of energy. A better opportunity presented itself and I would've been remiss to ignore it."

"Even if it means sucking the life-force from every living innocent angoli."

Shane threw his head back in a dramatic display. "If it means we'll be walking on the surface in ten years instead of a hundred, then so be it. However, without pure enzyme, we're all wasting our time."

Janet scrunched up her face. "You're getting plenty of pure enzyme-"

"Don't fool with me. The last batch was ineffective."

Janet clamped her mouth shut. Impossible! She'd

syphoned the enzyme from the harvest-bags herself. All two hundred thirty-five of them, including Cody's.

Could there be something wrong with Cody? She'd never forgive herself if her tests had somehow been causing him damage. What if his feedbags had been contaminated?

His feedbags. The storage cell. She searched the ground at her feet. The slow creep of dread rose up her spine and clung to her shoulders. Had Cody found a way to disrupt the harvest? She never should've given him that key! He seemed so sedate, though, so harmless.

"I await your explanation." Shane leaned back and studied her down his sharp nose.

Janet tried to regulate her breathing. "The harvest was fine. Your engineers must've contaminated the batch."

"Unlikely."

"Maybe you should spend more time supervising them, instead of harassing me."

Her wrist comms buzzed. She pulled it to her face. It read: "Alert: Breach in Central Lab."

Shane motioned to her wrist.

She swallowed hard. "It's nothing."

"You know I don't like secrets, Janet."

She clenched her hands into fists to keep them from shaking. "If you're done accusing me of this nonsense, I have work to do."

Shane leaned forward and pressed his palms against the desktop. His breath shot clouds of condensation across the glass. "If you fool with me, I will shut you down. I expect a full report of the last harvest on my desk by morning."

Janet whirled and strode out. Once around the corner, she broke into a run.

•   •   •

Janet shouldered through the lab doors and slid to a halt.

Cody sat in the middle of the room, white fur rustling beneath the overhead fan. Casual as could be. The door to his cage open. Down the hall, the other angoli whimpered and barked, a far cry from their typical vegetative state.

The doors swung shut behind her. Cody sat upright. He looked enormous without the bars separating them. His barrel chest and thick arms rippled with muscle. Arms that, without a thought, could crush a man. Or a woman. He kept his legs bent, poised. Legs that could leap the distance of the lab in a second. Gone was the sheen over his eyes and the clumsy gait. Cody was healthy. And he watched her.

"Hi, Cody," she said. Her vocal words meant nothing to him, but it beat just standing there. Her hands wouldn't stop shaking.

Cody motioned to her headgear tucked beneath her arm. She sucked in a breath. He wanted to talk. Good. She crept closer. He didn't look angry, but angoli expressions were elusive. She slowed just out of arm's reach.

The hell with it. She was one of them. He wouldn't hurt her. She closed the gap, until Cody's bulk loomed over her. Hot breath rustled her hair. She stood her ground, and handed him a fistful of cables. He connected the transmitting set to his forehand fingers, then slipped the receiving set beneath the mounds of flesh atop his forehead.

Janet pulled on her helmet and hit the power.

The doors banged open. Three men stormed in and fanned out, flechette pistols clutched in their grasps. Two pointed their guns at Cody, the third aiming at Janet's chest. They wore engineering coveralls, and looked familiar. She cursed herself for not remembering names, and for not caring enough to try. There were only a few hundred colonists, but after a while they all started to look the same.

One of them stepped forward. His finger twitched dangerously close to the trigger. "Looks like Shane was right. Traitorous bitch."

Janet held her hands out. "Just hold on, I can contain this-"

A black disk whizzed past her ear, and struck the man in the throat. The impact slammed him into the back wall with a sickening thud. The other two unloaded their weapons at Cody.

Janet swiveled. The angoli sailed through the air with the agility of a leopard, interface cables whipping behind him. His middle hands snatched the pistols, while his hind fists pounded into the men's midsections. They collapsed beneath Cody's weight, their bones crunching against the ground. A deep growl emanated from Cody's throat.

Janet stumbled backward and crashed into a terminal. She pressed a hand to her mouth and fought off a wave of nausea. An alarm blared down the halls of the habitat.

"Cody...no..."

Cody turned to face her. Blood streamed down his face from one of his receiving nodes. The cables were still attached, but the protective skin-flap was mangled, revealing soft flesh beneath.

He leapt at her. She tried to dodge, but he was

too quick. Massive limbs encircled her, pinning her arms to her torso and lifting her off the ground. His fur reeked of dirt and sweat. He stuck the barrels of both flechette pistols against her neck.

"Well, well."

Janet squirmed in Cody's grasp, craning her neck to catch sight of Shane in the doorway. He held a pistol in a casual grip, aimed at Cody.

His lip curled into a sneer. "Master and servant. Remind me which is which, again."

"Shane, don't hurt him-"

Shane spat. "You still think they're innocent. Foolish woman." He cocked his head. "Perhaps this is an opportunity to rid myself of you. Who's to say the beast didn't shoot you first, before I was able to slay it?"

Shane turned the gun on Janet and fired. She tried to scream, but the pressure against her chest pushed the air out silent. Cody twisted her, and the whole lab spun on its side. A burning lance struck her shoulder, and fire shot down her arm.

A groan echoed through the lab. Human. Metal struck flesh again and again, punctuated by the wet snapping of bones.

Janet slipped from Cody's arms and landed on the floor. Pain seared her shoulder, where a flechette dart was embedded all the way to the metal fins. Blood streamed down her bicep. She gritted her teeth and looked away.

Shane lay in a bloodied heap near the doors. Cody had upended the supply cabinet and was tearing through the contents. The cables were taut against his head and forehands. Overhead, alarms screamed.

"Cody..." She could hardly formulate a coherent thought through the pain.

Cody grabbed a fistful of items and leapt to Janet's side. Firm hands worked the flesh around her wound, and she let out a gasp. The room was filling with white flecks.

The cold nozzle of a jet injector pressed against her neck. It hissed. A tremor rippled down her spine, and the pain in her shoulder ebbed. Her vision returned in time to see Cody tying off her wound. The bloody flechette round lay discarded at his feet.

Janet looked up into his big purple eyes. He'd never been this close. His breath was hot against her face, and his scent invaded her nostrils.

"You will never be one of us."

Janet swallowed. "I'm your friend-"

"Friends do this?" Cody swept a middle hand across the lab. "You know nothing of my people. You tricked us, kept us weak and stupid. Maybe this is your way. It is not ours. I will let you live, but the others will die."

Cody tore the cables loose and tossed them to the floor.

She blinked back a flood of tears. "I'm sorry..."

He turned his back and leapt to the central console. With the precision of a surgeon, he flicked a keycard into the machine and tapped the screens. Down the hall, rows of cages swung open.

Janet gaped. He'd reprogrammed the keycard-but how?

He slipped the card beneath a fold of fur, and his forehand fingertips glistened in the overhead lighting. His neural transmitters, of course! Turned on the magnetically-programmed keycard, his fingers became hot-wiring cables. It would've required more than a cursory understanding of their systems, though. He'd been watching her. Who'd been performing tests on whom, these past months?

The angoli lumbered from their cages, swarming the central lab with barks and whines. One of them, a smaller female with a blue stripe along her side, darted over to Cody and pressed her fingers into his forehead. Cody reciprocated and their gazes met. Cody lowered his head and pressed his cheek into the female's neck.

Janet watched in silence. He always said he didn't have a mate. Maybe he'd just been protecting her from tests, or worse. Janet looked down at her hands, so small and soft. Cody was right. She'd never be one of them.

The angoli pair disentangled, then Cody stepped in front of the pack. He formed his hands into a series of shapes and the angoli erupted in a cacophony of howls. Janet pressed her hands over her ears. It was deafening. Cody led the pack tearing down the hallway toward the center of the habitat.

Janet sat up. Cody's words rang in her head. I will let you live, but the others will die. What a disgraceful double agent she'd been. She'd failed the angoli and now she'd secured a grisly fate for the colonists. The angoli would overwhelm them, would kill every last one of them-

Trilo. She struggled to her feet and snatched Shane's pistol. Clutching her bandaged arm close, she sprinted down the hall. The comms helmet still chafed against her temples, but there was no time to dislodge it. Cables streamed behind her like plastic dreadlocks. Up ahead, screams cut through the din of the alarm. An explosion rocked the building, sending rubble raining down.

Janet took the stairs in threes. She stumbled onto

the observation deck, panting. The night air felt thin in her lungs.

Skirmishes had broken out across the habitat. Human and angoli bodies stretched all the way to the perimeter. The habitat's shell buckled and cracked around mangled pylons. The main airlock was caved in, and Angol's atmosphere flooded through gaping holes.

Janet tried to regulate her breathing with long, deep breaths. The terraforming efforts had already bolstered the oxygen content of the outside atmosphere to around fifteen percent, but that was still low enough to limit activity. The nearest oxygen tanks were adjacent to the airlock, where-

Past the collapsed airlock, one of the laser-turrets turned. A white angoli manned the controls at the top. Cody.

He powered up the laser and unleashed a beam of fury across the shya fields. Rows of angoli tossed barrels of reserve fuel onto the fields, then dove for cover. Explosions lit the night sky. Flames ripped across the field and toward a thousand oxygen vents.

When the burning fuel reached the vents, massive geysers of fire erupted into the air. The ground shook. Janet lost her balance, slammed into the old comms array, then fell to the catwalk floor. She clutched the metal lattice as tremors ripped through the habitat. The catwalk bent and rumbled, but held.

She dragged herself to her feet. Outside, the entire shya field had collapsed into a single, vast sinkhole. Blackened stumps and shriveled vents stretched all the way to the coast.

Janet gripped the rail with white-knuckled hands. Cody had known exactly what to do. How long had he planned this? How many of his innocent questions had been calculated?

Flechette rounds thunked against the laser-turret's shielding. Through holes in the habitat, the colonists were unloading on Cody. The angoli swiveled. His eyes narrowed, and lips curled back. He ducked farther behind the shielding until only his head was visible. The laser bore down on the habitat.

"Cody, no!" Janet slammed her fists against the rail. The colonists reloaded and fired again. Trilo's scraggly beard stood out amongst the crowd. She pulled up her wrist and punched the comms.

"Trilo, run!"

The line scratched with interference, punctuated by flechette-fire.

"It's too late for that!" Trilo's voice was strained.

Cody's laser swept closer, already nearly at the perimeter. Once it reached the remaining fuel reserves...

Janet clenched her teeth and scanned the deck. Most of the equipment had broken loose and fallen during the explosion. All that remained was the old comms gear, a row of smart binoculars, and a terminal. Dammit!

She leaned over the rail. The cables of her helmet tangled around her face her, shrouding her vision. She grabbed them and started to yank.

She froze, cables still in hand, and shot a glance at Cody. The firelight glistened off his head-wound. The angoli could only communicate by touch, but one of Cody's receivers was exposed. A directed electromagnetic signal might substitute for a long cable. There was no telling whether the old comms gear was even operational, let alone capable of turning to the microwave band. But it was worth a shot.

"Trilo, hold your fire! You have to trust me."

Trilo cursed into the comms. "We need to kill it-
"

"Please! Let me fix this."

The gunfire stopped. "I hope you know what you're doing, babe."

No point in lying to him, so she said nothing. She ran to the terminal. The cables were slick with sweat in her hands as she jacked in. Her breath came in ragged heaves. She overrode the wavelength limiter and cranked the tuner to the correct band. Muscling the directional antenna from its housing, she propped it against the railing and turned it to face Cody.

She reached over to flip it on and the antenna slipped from her grip. It tumbled over the railing and fell toward the habitat floor. Janet lunged for the device. Her body slammed into the catwalk as her fingers closed around the antenna's trailing strap. It swung over the edge. She hauled it up and jammed it into her hip for stability. Taking aim at Cody's head, she switched it on.

Cody halted the tower's movement and turned his cold glare at Janet. She shuddered.

"Cody, please! Stop this."

He reached a forehand up to cover his exposed receiver.

"Wait! Let me talk."

He paused, then let his forehand drop. His other hands remained glued to the turret controls.

She swallowed. "These people aren't to blame. They were only following orders. If you want to blame anyone, it should be me. You were right; I didn't do everything I could."

Cody cocked his head.

"I saw you with your mate, in the lab. Down

there is mine. He's a good man, he doesn't deserve this. I'll do anything you ask, if you'll just spare his life. Please, Cody."

Cody dropped his gaze to the cluster of colonists below. Sweat and blood stained their faces. He turned back to Janet, thrusted a forehand in the direction of the colony ship.

Janet swallowed. The alarm wailed through the habitat. Their home. She looked beyond the perimeter. The pack of angoli stood at the base of the laser tower with knuckles down. Cody watched her with those eyes she'd studied for so long.

"I understand. We'll leave your planet and never return."

Cody rose to his hind legs and turned his back. He scampered down the ladder and joined the rest of the pack. Without another glance they tromped off into the night.

• • •

Janet crouched atop the scorched bluff and scanned the sinkhole that was once the shya fields. The breeze felt good against her skin. The air was thin, and in time, would be thinner still. Behind her, the colony ship's thrusters growled.

Something brushed against her arm. She looked up to see Trilo kneeling at her side. He'd shaved. His face looked bare and young. Like when they first met.

He skipped a rock across the blackened field.

"I'm sorry," he said. "You were right. About the angoli, about me. I just wanted this to work too much. I wanted to start a family here, with you."

Janet closed her eyes, they stung. "Me too. I

thought we could live together. Angoli and humans."

Trilo draped his arm over her shoulder. It was warm. It felt good, just resting there.

"You saved them," he said. "You did all you could."

Janet winced at his choice of words. "For a while there, I thought I was more angoli than human. Silly."

Trilo squeezed her shoulder and said nothing.

She looked at him. "Thank you for agreeing to leave."

Trilo chuckled. "It wasn't my choice. The project sustained losses well beyond Horizon Enterprises' failure threshold."

Janet clenched her teeth. Failure threshold. Lives lost. She threaded her fingers between Trilo's.

"Why'd they do it?" he asked. "Destroy the plants. Can they even survive, without them?"

Janet shook her head. She'd been asking herself the same question all day. "They'd rather take their chances on a damaged planet. Beats the option we gave them."

Trilo sighed. "Yeah."

They sat in silence, until the sun dipped to the horizon.

Trilo stood. "We'd better go, everyone's ready."

"I'll catch up."

He nodded, and left her alone atop the bluff.

She reached into her backpack and pulled out her old helmet. The cables dangled limp from all sides. She set it atop the highest rock facing the horizon. Facing Cody. She hung around for a few more minutes just staring across the fields. Hoping to see his face one more time.

Cody never showed.

Janet turned her back, and walked to the ship.

Douglas Owen

He is the Managing Editor of DAOwen Publications which holds the imprints Science Fiction and Fantasy Publications, Love Knot Books, Wicked Tales and Tumbleweed books. It was his desire to put forth a publication that would inspire people to let their muse wild. He is the author of the Spear series and Inside My Mind, a collection of short stories and flash fiction. His writing list is massive but that is what happens when you follow your dream, and that is what he is doing now. Doug offers this last story to round out the anthology with a strong lost friends theme.

Dirtside

A status light on the control panel turned from green to red. Another light turned red. The death of green lights happened all over the ship. It bathed the control room in an ambient glow of crimson.

The computer monitored the warning lights and sounded an alarm to start the reanimation process on Craig's cryogenic unit. As the internal temperature of the unit rose, the protective cover retracted to expose the face of a young boy no more than 10. With slow deliberation, the macro metre film that protected the child's body folded into the necklace he wore.

Craig moaned. His head pounded as he moved it

to the right. Air ruffed his hair. He opened his mouth and traced a dry tongue on cracked lips. The cover popped. Getting up ran through his mind but constricted muscles burned. With effort, he willed lifted both arms and grasped the bar. He pulled on it, and vomited bile.

A klaxon wailed. Craig rolled over. He jumped out of the unit and his foot slipped on the sick. The presence of high gravity confused him. He stood then stumbled to the control room. The red lights were not the only brightness in the room. The ship rocked.

Craig's head smacked against the control board. Blood trickled down his face. His gaze darted across the board. The view screen glowed with streaks of red fire. The ship plummeted through the atmosphere of a planet. The light-drive no longer bent space. Chemical rockets fired, pushing the ship forward. He braced, and noticed the chronometer on the board. 100 years.

Sickened, Craig strapped himself into the pilot seat. The roar of rockets was deafening. The ship jostled. The ship hurtled through the planet's atmosphere too fast. Heat built up and it became hard to breathe. He closed his eyes.

•   •   •

Eight more chemical rockets fired to slow the descent but it was not enough. The ship screamed as metal twisted from the impact. Craig strained against the straps. The torture of metal grinding rock went on forever. An air breach alarm split the chaos and a smell of sulphur hit him hard. Claws raked the inside of his throat.

The alarms stopped and lights went dark. He

could not see what was going on as the ship ground to a halt. Craig breathed a sigh of relief and believed he was safe. A creaking crescendoed as the ship tilted forward.

Craig was weightless. The ship fell, tumbled, and then it stopped.

•　　•　　•

Water struck Craig's face. A metallic taste filled his mouth. He glanced at the destruction in the upside-down ship. A large goose egg formed at his hairline. Pain lanced through his head.

Craig felt the water strike his face again. The metallic taste was back. He looked down, or up due to his orientation. A piece of a console's cover jutted out of his leg. Blood trickled down it and dripped toward his head. He screamed. The ripping pain from the puncture wound started to overpower the pounding ache from his head and the straps. The med kit was kept just under the console and he stretched to grab it. His fingers touched the kit then pulled it free. The clasp popped without issues, but he forgot to turn it around. The scissors and ampules spilled to the roof. The auto-injector was secured to the lid. He unsnapped it and dialled pain killer. With the injector pressed against his leg, he pushed the activation button. The needle delivered numbness.

The auto-injector fell to the roof. Craig relaxed for a few seconds, allowing his arms to swing free. He started to breathe easier, the pain subsided. Attached to the med kit lid was the skin sealing foam and he removed it from the case. With one hand he held the spray bottle and the other grasped the metal fragment. He took a deep breath and pulled.

Blood flowed out of the deep laceration. He sprayed the foam into the gash and the metal fragment dropped out of his hand. The blood stopped flowing. Fingers relaxed and the spray bottle fell to the roof as well. His gaze followed the can as it descended. It bounced six times before coming to a rest near the emergency exit. Craig sighed.

He relaxed, and tried not to be concerned. It was only a matter of time before he freed himself. The number 100 started to float around. Just a matter of time. 1200 months, 438,000 days. He opened the small pendant around his neck. His fingers traced the emblem of his house. That one thing his parents had given him before placing him on the emergency transport, promising to follow soon. He cracked it open and looked at the simple 2D pictures of his mother and father. Craig smiled at their little joke. An image easily created 500 years before any of their births was all he had to remember them by. He touched the picture of his mother.

"Craig, remember we love you. Our hearts are with you. Soon, we will be united once again. The rebels are about to breach the outer defenses and I need you safe. We are proud of you, son. I am proud of you."

The voice of his mother echoed in his ears. How long had she been dead now? It will depend on what happened after they had shuffled him into the emergency ship. Did they grieve for him? Was there even a funeral or did they refuse to give up hope? They had arranged the fast mover for him, but who programmed it? 24 days. That's all he should have been in suspension for, not 100 years.

His stomach growled and the bump on his head throbbed. He had to get out of the chair. With one hand he pulled the latch, and fell.

The roof was pure metal. He hit hard. The floor of the control room showed glowing arrows pointing to escape pods. Why had they insisted on him travelling alone? Blackness engulfed him.

•   •   •

Craig stirred, lifted himself up and crawled through the bulkhead. The corridor was dark, and he could just see the other partition 15 metres away. Food would be there. It had been a day since he awoke, and now the need for nourishment ached within.

The next bulkhead loomed before him. Darkness stared back. A foreboding curtain of black. Nothing could be used for a light source, so he hefted himself up over the bulkhead's opening and into the blackness. Feet crunched against something unseen. He groped with his hands, pushing hard metal objects aside while making his way toward the wall where the emergency rations would be kept.

A red light blinked twice. He reached for it, grasping at the spot he saw the blink of hope. Or was it a curse of death? It blinked again. His hand grasped the object and he pulled a small box free. He touched a panel with his other hand. It moved aside and packet after packet of emergency rations toppled over him. He managed to grasp several before he made his way to the hatch. That dim opening promised life.

He crawled through it and made his way back to the control room. His leg only showed a thick red line where the jagged metal had once protruded. The bio-gel had healed his leg just as it was designed to. Knitting muscles and skin together. His hand dropped the packages once he reached the control room and he sat down.

The box blinked again. ETB marked the sides. Emergency Transmission Beacon. There was no switch, lever or button to turn it off. The case was designed to survive a planet side crash. Case hardened neutronium. Harder than diamond. It blinked again.

Slowly Craig placed the box on the floor. It survived 100 years. He survived 100 years.

Craig cried.

•   •   •

It was three months since his crash and no one had come to find him. Craig chewed the biscuit and drank the water from the last survival pack. He could survive the planet, but only just. The air was the hardest. The presence of sulphur burned his lungs a little each time he breathed.

He had wired up the solar generators and given the ship a little life. The main computer ran from sun up to sun down. Six hours. Nothing more. Night lasted longer. 12 hours. The sounds of animals screaming in the wilderness from the outside disturbed him for the first two weeks, but Craig became used to them.

Most of the life on the planet comprised of reptiles and birds. Both carried impressive teeth and claws.

The last of the rations disappeared into his mouth.

"Program complete," the computer sounded.

Craig looked up and moved to the panel. He had pulled it down from the main control and set it up near where he slept. A program to purify rainwater had finished, and the computer displayed the materials. It will be a large project, but he felt up to the challenge. His thoughts turned to the survival training pounded into him for years …

"Craig! Use a stone to separate the bark from the tree." Dennison smashed a rock against the tree, pulverizing it. The line stretched for a meter and a half. His fingers pulled the top layer of bark away from the tree revealing the phloem. He started to create rope. "You boil the water and soak the bark. The fibres will separate and you can use them to make the string."

Craig watched the man work, and wondered how long it would take his six year old hands to do what a practiced veteran could. He mimicked the same movements, ripped the bark away, and created the rope as Dennison had.

The old Sargent at Arms smiled down at Craig. "You have done well."

An arrow struck the bird in the chest. It fell to the ground.

Craig ran to the carcase then scooped it up before any of the larger birds noticed what had happened. He moved quickly, and soon was back at the ship.

It did not take him long to pull the feathers off or extract the arrow and remove the innards. The process was laborious, but needed. After an hour he started cooking.

He pulled off his shirt. It did not fit as well as it had when he landed on the planet. The tightness across his chest was uncomfortable, and the sleeves cut into his arms. Craig had grown a lot from the constant exercise of just staying alive. This planet was hostile.

Craig named most of the birds he had seen over the last few months. There were the small birds with green and blue feathers. He called them screamers. They made the loudest noise when other birds came close. Craig caught one once, but it hardly had any flesh on the bones. Swoppers were different. They flew fast and attacked other bird's nests to steal eggs. The one he caught yielded a lot of meat, but it tasted strange and was through his body fast.

Craig usually tried to get the birds he called gawkers. They sat in the trees looking down at the small animals that ran around the forest floor. Gawkers tasted the best.

"Remember to only eat a small amount," the Sargent at Arms had told him. "That way if you have a reaction it will be small. Test everything. Most planets that you can live on offer a lot of food to help you live. Everything has protein and carbs. Learn what you can eat. But if you have one, use the scanner to tell you if you can eat it."

That day, Dennis had taught him how to use a scanner, and how to use his head.

The computer voice sounded from inside the ship. "Schematic complete."

He stood. The bird would take a while to cook, and nothing came near the ship any more. Craig went inside and climbed the ropes to the terminal three metres above. "Display," he said.

The screen came alive with the digital schematic of a pulse scanner. Parts of the ship would be needed, but nothing he couldn't do without. He read off the parts, and ticked the mental check-list, identifying where each part was. The only problem, he didn't know where to find one of the metal pieces needed. And if he was going to identify any ship approaching the planet, he needed this thin strip of metal.

"Ship, where can I find this?"

"Carbon electorate can be manufactured with the components found on the ship. A detailed listing will follow. Steps will be laid out for you."

Craig knew enough not to argue with the computer. This was all it would say for now, and it would take him a long time to find out more. "Is it a long process?"

"Negative."

He climbed down from the station and started to gather the parts. Soon his arms were full, and he made his way outside to start the construction. This would not be one of those small hand held units he had learned on. No, it was going to be big. There was nothing that he could do about it.

"Remember to ground yourself before applying power," the computer said. "An electrical accident could render you unconscious for several hours, and nightfall is approaching."

He ignored the obvious. The ship still treated him like he was a child, and not a survivor. Half way through building the scanner he looked up to see a small quadruped staring at him. It was a ghastly sight. The animal stood just under a metre tall with leathery skin that covered a bony body. The snout resembled an ape's mouth, but the ears were similar to a cat. Large fangs fell centimetres past the drooling mouth and hand like paws adorned the limbs. The animal let out a pitiful whine.

Craig froze.

"Animals on our planet rarely attack humans. On some planets they will be curious, but most small ones will run from you." Dennison paced the practice yard and smiled. Craig stood frozen in place, watching the large cat sniff the air. "Show no fear when confronted by a predator. Control your breathing and it may soon lose interest in you. That is when you can either attack or escape. Usually escape is the best choice, but that will depend on how hungry either you or it is."

Craig was not hungry. The creature looked famished.

The animal sniffed the air, turned its head and whimpered again.

"Don't eat me and I'll feed you," Craig said.

The creature took a step forward. It sniffed the air again.

"Okay. Since you're not afraid of me, and I'm not afraid of you. How about I just move my hand …"

Two green eyes shifted their gaze to him, and he stopped moving.

"I have food here. Are you hungry?"

The animal's mouth opened and the longest tongue Craig had ever seen lolled out, stopping just three centimetres from the ground.

"Wow! Bet that makes it easy to clean your ears." He swore the creature smiled at him. "Okay. I'll just reach back here …" Craig reached into his back pocket and pulled out some dried meat. The creature pulled its tongue back into a slobbering mouth and sniffed the air again. "Here you go."

Craig tossed the meat toward the animal's feet. It watched the food arc through the air. The action was faster than he could have imagined. The creature snapped the meat out of the air and swallowed. He caught a glimpse of the teeth. Each row looked sharper than needles.

"Okay. I'll keep you fed and you don't bite me. Sound good?"

The quadruped shifted forward and sniffed the air again. Craig took out another piece of meat and threw it toward the creature. It snapped the meat out of the air again and swallowed. Craig watched as it cocked its head sideways a little and panted.

"If you want more you'll have to come inside for it." Craig motioned toward the ship. The creature walked forward and stopped beside him. It turned its head and glared at him, then leaned toward him. Craig let the thing lean against him and slowly brought up his hand to pet it. "I guess you're as lonely as I am."

Even with the bones protruding from its sides, the animal was muscle. Each rib stood out, but between them pulsed power.

Keeping his hand on the beast, Craig started to walk toward the ship. It followed him with obedience.

•   •   •

The stone sailed through the air as a missile flies into the sky. The swooper's head turned, but not enough. The stone struck it on the side of the head. The bird did not scream. The bird did not squawk. The bird stopped flapping its wings and fell to the ground.

A large quadruped ran with a looping gate toward the fallen bird and stopped when it reached the body. It sniffed and rolled out a long thick tongue which it wrapped around the still body and lifted it to the awaiting mouth. The creature did not eat it, but gently squeezed until it held the carcass firm. Then it turned and ran back the way it came.

•   •   •

Craig stood by the ship and watched Bob run toward him with the bird in his mouth. He smiled. It had taken him a week to train the creature not to eat the bird before bringing it to him. He called the animal Bob, after the pet that died more than 100 years ago.

"Good boy," Craig said. He reached out to take the large bird, but Bob stepped back a little. "Come on, no fooling. I'm hungry and so are you. I have to clean and cook it before dark comes."

The animal stretched back with its haunches in the air. It let go of the bird and stood back up, rolling the carcass forward. Bob shook his body.

"Funny, Bob." He bent over and picked up the bird. "We eat good tonight."

•   •   •

Craig sat back from the jumble of metal with a thin black wire in his hand. Bob lay beside him, tongue rolled out in the dirt. The quadruped's eyes watched with longing.

"This is it, Bob. I put power to this and if there's anyone from the Royal Guards within a 100 parsec, they'll come running." He reached behind and fumbled for the small disk. After a few seconds he looked back, saw the glint and wrapped his fingers around it. "This better work, Bob. We only have three of these and this thing will burn one out if there's a short."

He pushed the small disk into a holder. The black wire hovered there in his hand, just a centimetre away from the contact. Bob pulled his tongue back into his mouth and raised his head. Black eyebrows lifted over yellow eyes.

"Here goes nothing," Craig said, and touched the wire to the contact.

Lights blinked and a pinging sound repeated every three seconds. Craig smiled at Bob. "I did it!"

Bob turned his head sideways and knotted his brow.

"The transponder is working. I thought something didn't go right, but here we are, waiting for someone to answer. See that light right there?" Craig pointed. Bob followed the finger. "If someone receives it, that light will turn yellow. But if it turns red ... Well, it'll be someone else."

The light flickered yellow.

Craig could not believe his eyes. Yellow. They found him. The Royal Guard will show up soon. He will be off this planet and home soon.

The light flickered red. Then yellow. Then back to red.

The flashing of the colors gave him a headache. The light went back and forth from yellow to red and back again. It danced an interplay of color and Bob just stared at it. Craig got up and strode into the ship and put the computer onto a new problem. Protection.

•   •   •

"I'm not ready!" Craig ran from the bridge to the medical bay, jumping over the garbage strewn about. "Bob! Where are you?"

The sound of a ship entering the atmosphere erupted through the forest. Craig stopped and waited.

Another boom caused the ground to shake, followed by the sound of pulse lasers reaching out to destroy another. Lights flashed in the sky. Fingers of death reached out from each ship, trying to punch a hole through the armour of each other.

"Bob! Where are you, boy? Get in here!" Craig stopped just before the hibernation chamber, not knowing what to do. He waited, and the sound of a ship crashing echoed in the distance. "Their reactor will go critical soon. Unless they are the rebellion, then the Royal Guard will encompass the ship with a dampening field. Come on, Bob, we need to get into the protective shield of the sleeper." If he waited and it was not the rebels, then the blast would kill him.

"Bob," he whispered, and took one last glance around before sealing himself into the chamber, touching his pendant and allowing sleep to take him away.

The Unbound anthology publishes yearly. Each anthology is theme based and announced prior to the opening of the submission period.

This is the first in the anthology. Unbound I: Lost Friends was announced in January 2015. The theme lost friends became open to only Science Fiction short stories ranging between 3,000 and 20,000 words. Each author who is picked for the anthology receives a small payment for publication and royalties on the sales.

If you are interested in writing for this anthology please see our web page on how to submit at:

http://scififantasypublications.com

We also have a horror anthology called Muffled Scream which publishes annually. You can find out more about that publication from their website:

http://wickedtales.ca

The Muffled Scream anthology is also theme based.

Tumbleweed Books publishes an anthology of feel good stories in their Love of Life anthology. More information can be found at:

http://tumbleweedbooks.ca

We hope you enjoyed this publication. For more fine works please see our online store or your nearest book store.

https://daowenpublications.ca

www.ingramcontent.com/pod-product-compliance
Lightning Source LLC
Chambersburg PA
CBHW061212170626
46809CB00003B/1323